Charles Dickens

Charles Dickens's new Christmas Story

Mrs. Lirriper's Lodgings

Charles Dickens

Charles Dickens's new Christmas Story
Mrs. Lirriper's Lodgings

ISBN/EAN: 9783337379759

Printed in Europe, USA, Canada, Australia, Japan

Cover: Foto ©Andreas Hilbeck / pixelio.de

More available books at **www.hansebooks.com**

CHARLES DICKENS'S

NEW

CHRISTMAS STORY.

M^{RS} LIRRIPER'S LODGINGS.

MOBILE, ALA.:

PRINTED AT THE OFFICE OF THE DAILY ADVERTISER AND REGISTER.

1864.

I.

HOW MRS. LIRRIPER CARRIED ON THE BUSINESS.

WHOEVER would begin to be worried with letting Lodgings that wasn't a lone woman with a living to get is a thing inconceivable to me my dear, excuse the familiarity but it comes natural to me in my own little room when wishing to open my mind to those that I can trust and I should be truly thankful if they were all mankind but such is not so, for have but a Furnished bill in the window and your watch on the mantlepiece and farewell to it if you turn your back but for a second however gentlemanly the manners, nor is being of your own sex any safeguard as I have reason in the form of sugar-tongs to know, for that lady (and a fine woman she was) got me to run for a glass of water on the plea of going to be confined, which certainly turned out true but it was in the Station-House.

Number Eighty-one Norfolk Street Strand—situated midway between the City and St. James's and within five minutes' walk of the principal places of public amusement—is my address. I have rented this house many years as the parish rate-books will testify and I could wish my landlord was as alive to the fact as I am myself, but no bless you not a half a pound of paint to save his life nor so much my dear as a tile upon the roof though on your bended knees.

My dear you never have found Number Eighty-one Norfolk Street Strand advertised in Bradshaw's Railway Guide and with the blessing of Heaven you never will or shall so find it. Some there are who do not think it lowering themselves to make their names that cheap and even going the lengths of a portrait of the house not like it with a blot in every window and a coach and four at the door, but what will suit Wozenham's lower down on the other side of the way will not suit me, Miss Wozenham having her opinions and me having mine, though when it comes to systematic underbidding capable of being proved on oath in a court of justice and taking the form of "If Mrs. Lirriper names eighteen shillings a week, I name fourteen and six" it then comes to a settling self and your conscience as to argument your house to

I am well aware it is not or my opinion of you would be greatly lowered, and as to airy bedrooms and a night-porter in constant attendance the less said the better, the bedrooms being stuffy and the porter stuff.

It is forty years ago since me and my poor Lirriper got married at St. Clement's Danes where I now have a sitting in a very pleasant pew with genteel company and my own hassock and being partial to evening service not too crowded. My poor Lirriper was a handsome figure of a man with a beaming eye and a voice as mellow as a musical instrument made of honey and steel, but he had ever been a free liver being in the commercial traveling line and traveling what he called a limekiln road—"a dry road, Emma my dear," my poor Lirriper says to me "where I have to lay the dust with one drink or another all day long and half the night, and it wears me Emma"—and this led to his running through a good deal and might have run through the turnpike too when that dreadful horse that never would stand still for a single instant set off, but for its being night and the gate shut and consequently took his wheel my poor Lirriper and the gig smashed to atoms and never spoke afterwards. He was a handsome figure of a man and a man with a jovial heart and a sweet temper, but if they had come up then they never could have given you the mellowness of his voice and indeed I consider photographs wanting in mellowness as a general rule and making you look like a new-ploughed field.

My poor Lirriper being behindhand with the world and being buried at Hatfield church in Hertfordshire, not that it was his native place but that he had a liking for the Salisbury Arms where we went upon our wedding-day and passed as happy a fortnight as ever happy was, I went round to the creditors and I says "Gentlemen I am acquainted with the fact that I am not answerable for my late husband's debts but I wish to pay them for I am his lawful wife and his good name is dear to me. I am going into the business as a business and if I make it a success that my late husband for the sake of the love I bore him. " It took a long time to do but it was done, and the silver cream-jug which is between ourselves and the bed and the mattress in my room up-stairs (or it would have found legs so sure as ever the Furnished bill was up) being presented by the gentlemen engraved "To Mrs. Lirriper a mark of grateful respect for her honorable conduct" gave me a turn which was too much for my feelings, till Mr. Betley which at that time had the parlours and loved his joke says "Cheer up Mrs. Lirriper, you should feel as if it was only your christening and they were your godfathers and godmothers which did promise for you." And it brought me round, and I don't mind confessing to you my dear that I then put a sandwich and a drop of sherry in a little basket and went down to Hatfield churchyard outside the coach and kissed my hand and laid it with a kind of a proud and swelling love on my husband's grave, though bless you it had taken me so long to clear his name that my wedding ring was worn quite fine and smooth when I laid it on the green green waving grass.

I am an old woman now and my good looks are gone but that's me my dear over the plate-warmer and considered like in the times when you used to pay two guineas on ivory and took your chance pretty much how you came out, which made you very careful how you left it about afterwards because people were turned so red and uncomfortable by mostly guessing it was somebody else quite different, and there was once a certain person that had put his money in a hop business that came in one morning to pay his rent and his respects being the second floor that would have taken it down from its hook and put it in his breast pocket—you understand my dear—for the L, he says, of the original—only there was no mellowness in his voice and I wouldn't let him, but his opinion of it you may gather from his saying to it "Speak to me Emma!" which was far from a rational observation no doubt but still a tribute to its being a likeness, and I think myself it was like me when I was young and wore that sort of stays.

But it was about the Lodgings that I was intending to hold forth and certainly I ought to know something of the business having been in it so long, for it was early in the second year of my married life that I lost my poor Lirriper and I set up at Islington directly afterwards and afterwards came here, being two houses and eight and thirty years and some losses and a deal of experience.

Girls are your first trial after fixtures and they try you even worse than what I call the Wandering Christians, though why they should roam the earth looking for bills and then coming in and viewing the apartments and stickling about terms and never at all wanting them or dreaming of taking them being already provided, is a mystery I should be thankful to have explained if by any miracle it could be. It's wonderful they live so long and thrive so on it but I suppose the exercise makes it healthy, knocking so much and going from house to house and up and down stairs all day, and then their pretending to be so particular and punctual is a most astonishing thing, looking at their watches and saying "Could you give me the refusal of the rooms till twenty minutes past eleven the day after to-morrow in the forenoon, and supposing it to be considered essential by my friend from the country could there be a small iron bedstead put in the little room upon the stairs?" Why when I was new to it my dear I used to consider before I promised and to make my mind anxious with calculations and to get quite wearied out with disappointments, but now I says "Certainly by all means" well knowing it's a Wandering Christian and I shall hear no more about it, indeed by this time I know most of the Wandering Christians by sight as well as they know me, it being the habit of each individual revolving round London in that capacity to come back about twice a year, and it's very remarkable that it runs in families, and the children grow up to it, but even were it otherwise I should no sooner hear of the friend from the country which is a certain sign that I should nod and say to myself You're a Wandering Christian, though whether they are (as I have heard) persons of small property with a taste for regular employment and frequent change of scene I cannot undertake to tell you.

Girls as I was beginning to remark are one of your first and your lasting troubles, being like your teeth which begin with convulsions and never cease tormenting you from the time you cut them till they cut you, and then you don't want to part with them which seems hard but we must all succumb or buy artificial, and even where you get a will nine times out of ten you'll get a dirty face with it, and naturally lodgers do not like good society to be shown in with a smear of black across the nose or a smudgy eyebrow. Where they pick the black up is a mystery I cannot solve, as in the case of the willingest girl that ever came into a house half starved poor thing, a girl so willing that I called her Willing Sophy down upon her knees scrubbing early and late and ever cheerful but always smiling with a black face. And I says to Sophy "Now Sophy my good girl have a regular day for your stoves and keep the width of the Airy between yourself and the blacking and do not brush your hair with the bottoms of the saucepans and do not meddle with the snuffs of the candles and it stands to reason that it can no longer be" yet there it was and always on her nose, which turning up and being broad at the end seemed to boast of it and caused warning from a steady gentleman and excellent lodger with breakfast by the week but a little irritable and use of a sitting-room when required, his words being "Mrs. Lirriper I have arrived at the point of admitting that the Black is a man and a brother, but only in a natural form and when it can't be got off." Well consequently I put poor Sophy on to other work and forbid her answering the door or answering a bell on any account but she was so unfortunately willing that nothing would stop her flying up the kitchen stairs whenever a bell was heard to tingle. I put it to her "Oh Sophy Sophy for goodness goodness sake where does it come from?" To which that poor unlucky willing mortal bursting out crying to see me so vexed replied "I took a deal of black into me ma'am when I was a small child being much neglected and I think it must be, that it works out," so it continuing to work out of that poor thing and not having another fault to find with her I says Sophy "what do you seriously think of my helping you away to New South Wales where it might not be noticed?" Nor did I ever repent the money which was well spent, for she married the ship's cook on the voyage (himself a Mulotter) and did well and lived happy, and so far as ever I heard it was not noticed in a new state of society to her dying day.

In what way Miss Wozenham lower down on the other side of the way reconciled it to her feelings as a lady (which she is not) to entice Mary Anne Perkinsop from my service is best known to herself, I do not know and I do not wish to know how opinions are formed at Wozenham's on any point. But Mary Anne Perkinsop although I behaved handsomely to her and she behaved unhandsomely to me was worth her weight in gold as overawing lodgers without driving them away, for lodgers would be far more sparing of their bells with Mary Anne than I ever knew them be with Maid or Mistress, which is a great triumph especially when accompanied with a cast in the eye and a bag of bones, but it was the steadiness of her way with them through her father's having failed in Pork. It was Mary Anne's looking so re̶s̶p̶e̶c̶t̶a̶b̶l̶e̶ ̶i̶n̶ ̶h̶e̶r person and being so strict in her s̶p̶i̶r̶i̶t̶s̶ ̶c̶o̶n̶-̶ quered the ten-and-sixp̶e̶n̶c̶e̶ ̶g̶e̶n̶t̶l̶e̶m̶a̶n̶ ̶o̶r̶ ̶h̶e̶ weighed them both in a pair of s̶c̶a̶l̶e̶s̶ ̶e̶v̶e̶r̶y̶ morning) that I have ever had to d̶e̶a̶l̶ ̶w̶i̶t̶h̶ ̶a̶n̶d no lamb grow meeker, still it r̶e̶q̶u̶i̶r̶e̶d̶ ̶

round to me that Miss Wozenham happening to pass and seeing Mary Anne take in the milk of a milkman that made free in a rosy-faced way (I think no worse of him) with every girl in the street but was quite frozen up like the statue at Charing Cross by her, saw Mary Anne's value in the lodging business and went as high as one pound per quarter more, consequently Mary Anne with not a word betwixt us says "If you will provide yourself Mrs. Lirriper in a month from this day I have already done the same," which hurt me and I said so, and she then hurt me more by insinuating that her father having failed in Pork had laid her open to it.

My dear I do assure you it's a harassing thing to know what kind of girls to give the preference to, for if they are lively they get bell'd off their legs and if they are sluggish you suffer from it yourself in complaints and if they are sparkling-eyed they get made love to and if they are smart in their persons they try on your Lodger's bonnets and if they are musical I defy you to keep them away from bands and organs, and allowing for any difference you like in their heads their heads will be always out of window just the same And then what the gentlemen like in girls the ladies don't, which is fruitful hot water for all parties, and then there's temper though such a temper as Caroline Maxey's I hope not often. A good-looking black-eyed girl was Caroline and a comely made girl to your cost when she did break out and laid about her, as took place first and last through a new-married couple come to see London in the first floor and the lady very high and it was supposed not liking the good looks of Caroline having none of her own to spare, but anyhow she did try Caroline though that was no excuse. So one afternoon Caroline comes down into the kitchen flushed and flashing, and she says to me "Mrs. Lirriper that woman in the first has aggravated me past bearing," I says "Caroline keep your temper," Caroline says with a curdling laugh "Keep my temper? You're right Mrs. Lirriper, so I will. Capital D her !" bursts out Caroline (you might have struck me into the centre of the earth with a feather when she said it) "I'll give her a touch of the temper that I keep !" Caroline downs with her hair my dear, screeches and rushes up stairs, I following as fast as my trembling legs could bear me, but before I got into the room the dinner cloth and pink and white service all dragged off upon the floor with a crash and the new-married couple on their backs in the fire-grate, him with the shovel and tongs and a dish of cucumber across him and a merry it was summer-time. "Caroline" I says "be calm," but she catches off my cap and tears it in her teeth as she passes me, then pounces on the new married lady makes her a bundle of ribbons takes her by the two ears and knocks the back of her head upon the carpet Murder screaming all the time Policemen running down the street and Wozenham's windows (judge of my feelings when I came to know it) thrown up and Miss Wozenham calling out from the balcony with crocodile's tears "It's Mrs. Lirriper been overcharging somebody to madness — she'll be murdered — I always thought so—Pleeseman save her!" My dear four of them and Caroline behind the chiffoniere attacking with the poker and when disarmed prize fighting with her double fists, and down and up and up and down and dreadful! But I couldn't bear to see the poor young creature rough handled and her hair torn when they got the better of her, and I says "Gentlemen Policemen pray remember that her sex is the sex of your mothers and sisters and your sweethearts, and God bless them and you!" And there she was sitting down on the ground handcuffed, taking breath against the skirting-board and them cool with their coats in strips, and all she says was "Mrs. Lirriper I am sorry as ever I touched *you*, for you're a kind motherly old thing," and it made me think that I had often wished I had been a mother indeed and how would my heart have felt if I had been the mother of that girl! Well you know it turned out at the Police-office that she had done it before, and she had her clothes away and was sent to prison, and when she was to come out I trotted off to the gate in the evening with just a morsel of jelly in that little basket of mine to give her a mite of strength to face the world again, and there I met with a very decent mother waiting for her son through bad company and a stubborn one he was with his half boots not laced. So out came Caroline and I says "Caroline come along with me and sit down under the wall where it's retired and eat a little trifle that I have brought with me to do you good" and she throws her arms round my neck and says sobbing "O why were you never a mother when there are such mothers as there are!" she says, and in a half a minute more she begins to laugh and says "Did I really tear your cap to shreds?" and when I told her "You certainly did so Caroline" she laughed again and said while she patted my face "Then why do you wear such queer old caps you dear old thing? If you hadn't worn such queer old caps I don't think I should have done it even then." Fancy the girl! Nothing could get out of her what she was going to do except O she would do well enough, and we parted she being very thankful and kissing my hands, and I never more saw or heard of that girl, except I shall always believe that a very genteel cap which was

brought anonymous to me one Saturday night in an oil-skin basket by a most impertinent young sparrow of a monkey whistling with dirty shoes on the clean steps and playing the harp on the Airy railings with a hoop-stick came from Caroline.

What you lay yourself open to my dear in the way of being the object of uncharitable suspicions when you go into the Lodging business I have not the words to tell you, but never was I so dishonourable as to have two keys nor would I willingly think it even of Miss Wozenham, lower down on the other side of the way sincerely hoping that it may not be, though doubtless at the same time money cannot come from nowhere and it is not reason to suppose that Bradshaws put it in for love be it blotty as it may. It *is* a hardship hurting to the feelings that Lodgers open their minds so wide to the idea that you are trying to get the better of them and shut their minds so close to the idea that they are trying to get the better of you, but as Major Jackman says to me "I know the ways of this circular world Mrs. Lirriper, and that's one of 'em all round it" and many is the little ruffle in my mind that the Major has smoothed, for he is a clever man who has seen much. Dear dear, thirteen years have passed though it seems but yesterday since I was sitting with my glasses on at the open front parlour window one evening in August (the parlours being then vacant) reading yesterday's paper my eyes for print being poor though still I am thankful to say a long sight at a distance, when I hear a gentleman come posting across the road and up the streets in a dreadful rage talking to himself in a fury and d'ing and c'ing somebody. "By George!" says he out loud and clutching his walking-stick, "I'll go to Mrs. Lirriper's. Which is Mrs. Lirriper's?" Then looking round and seeing me he flourishes his hat right off his head as if I had been the queen and he says "Excuse the intrusion Madam, but pray Madam can you tell me at what number in this street there resides a well-known and much-respected lady by the name of Lirriper?" A little flustered though I must say gratified I took off my glasses and curtseyed and said "Sir, Mrs. Lirriper is your humble servant." "As-tonishing!" said he. "A million pardons! Madam, may I ask you to have the kindness to direct one of your domestics to open the door to a gentleman in search of apartments, by the name of Jackman?" I had never heard the name but a politer gentleman I never hope to see, for says he "Madam I am shocked at your opening the door yourself to no worthier fellow than Jemmy Jackman. After you Madam. I never precede a lady." Then he comes into the parlours and he sniffs and he says "Hah! These are parlours! Not musty cupboards" he says "but parlours, and no smell of coal-sacks." Now my dear it having been remarked by some inimical to the whole neighbourhood that it always smells of coal-sacks which might prove a drawback to Lodgers if encouraged, I says to the Major gently though firmly that I think he is referring to Arundel or Surrey or Howard but not Norfolk. "Madam" says he "I refer to Wozenham's lower down over the way—Madam you can form no notion what Wozenham's is—Madam it is a vast coal-sack, and Miss Wozenham has the principles and manners of a female heaver—Madam from the manner in which I have heard her mention you I know she has no appreciation of a lady, and from the manner in which she has conducted herself towards me I know she has no appreciation of a gentleman——Madam my name is Jackman—should you require any other reference than what I have already said, I name the Bank of England—perhaps you know it!" Such was the beginning of the Major's occupying the parlours and from that hour to this the same and a most obliging Lodger and punctual in all respects except one irregular which I need not particularly specify, but made up for by his being a protection and at all times ready to fill in the papers of the Assessed Taxes and Juries and that, and once collared a young man with the drawing-room clock under his cloak, and once on the parapets with his own hands and blankets put out the kitchen chimney and afterwards attending the summons made a most eloquent speech against the Parish before the magistrates and saved the engine, and ever quite the gentleman though passionate. And certainly Miss Wozenham's detaining the trunks and umbrella was not in a liberal spirit though it may have been according to her rights in law or an act I would myself have stooped to, the Major being so much the gentleman that though he is far from tall he seems almost so when he has his shirt frill out and his frock-coat on and his hat with the curly brims, and in what service he was I cannot truly tell you my dear whether Militia or Foreign, for I never heard him even name himself as Major but always simple "Jemmy Jackman" and once soon after he came when I felt it my duty to let him know that Miss Wozenham had put it about that ho was no Major and I took the liberty of adding "which you are sir" his words were "Madam at any rate I am not a Minor, and sufficient for the day is the evil thereof" which cannot be denied to be the sacred truth, nor yet his military ways of having his boots with only the dirt brushed off taken to him in the front parlour every morning on a clean plate and varnishing them himself with a little sponge and a saucer and a whistle in a whisper

so sure as ever his breakfast is ended, and so neat his ways that it never soils his linen which is scrupulous though more in quality than quantity, neither that nor his moustachios which to the best of my belief are done at the same time and which are as black and shining as his boots, his head of hair being a lovely white.

It was the third year nearly up of the Major's being in the parlours that early one morning in the month of February when Parliament was coming on and you may therefore suppose a number of impostors were about ready to take hold of anything they could get, a gentleman and lady from the country came in to view the Second, and I well remember that I had been looking out of window and had watched them and the heavy sleet driving down the street together looking for bills. I did not quite take to the face of the gentleman though he was good-looking too but the lady was a very pretty young thing and delicate, and it seemed too rough for her to be out at all though she had only come from the Adelphi Hotel which would have not been much above than a quarter of a mile if the weather had been less severe. Now it did so happen my dear that I had been forced to put five shillings weekly additional on the second in consequence of a loss from running away full-dressed as if going out to a dinner party, which was very artful and had made me rather suspicious taking it along with Parliament, so when the gentleman proposed three months certain and the money in advance and leave then reserved to renew on the same terms for six months more, I says I was not quite certain but that I might have engaged myself to another party but would I step down stairs and look into it if they would take a seat. They took a seat and I went down to the handle of the Major's door that I had already begun to consult finding it a great blessing, and I knew by his whistling in a whisper that he was varnishing his boots which was generally considered private, however he kindly calls out 'If it's you, Madam, come in," and I went in and told him.

"Well Madam," says the Major rubbing his nose — as I did fear at the moment with the black sponge but it was only his knuckle, he being always neat and dexterous with his fingers—"well, Madam, I suppose you would be glad of the money?"

I was delicate of saying "Yes" too out, for a little extra colour rose into the Major's cheeks and there was irregularity which I will not particularly specify in a quarter which I will not name.

"I am of opinion, Madam," says the Major "that when money is ready for you—when it is ready for you Mrs. Lirriper—you ought to take it. What is there against it, Madam, in this case up-stairs?"

"I really cannot say there is anything against it sir, still I thought I would consult you."

"You said a newly-married couple, I think, Madam," says the Major.

I says "Ye-es. Evidently. And indeed the young lady mentioned to me in a casual way that she had not been married many months."

The Major rubbed his nose again and stirred the varnish round and round in its little saucer with his piece of sponge and took to his whistling in a whisper for a few moments. Then he says "You would call it a Good Let, Madam?"

"Oh certainly a Good Let sir."

"Say they renew for the additional six months. Would it put you about very much Madam if—if the worst was to come to the worst?" said the Major.

"Well I hardly know," I says to the Major. "It depends upon circumstances. Would you object sir for instance?"

"I?" says the Major. "Object? Jemmy Jackman? Mrs. Lirriper close with the proposal."

So I went up-stairs and accepted, and they came in next day which was Saturday and the Major was so good as to draw up a Memorandum of an agreement in a beautiful round hand and expressions that sounded to me equally legal and military, and Mr. Edson signed it on the Monday morning and the Major called upon Mr. Edson on the Tuesday and Mr. Edson called upon the Major on the Wednesday and the Second and the parlours were as friendly as could be wished.

The three months paid for had run out and we had got without any fresh overtures as to payment into May my dear, when there came an obligation upon Mr Edson to go on business expedition right across the Isle of Man, which fell quite unexpected on that pretty little thing and is not a place that according to my views is particularly in the way or anywhere at any time but that may be a matter of opinion. So short a notice was it that he was to go next day, and dreadfully she cried poor pretty and I am sure I cried too when I saw her on the cold pavement in the sharp east wind—it being a very backward spring that year—taking a last leave of him with her pretty bright hair blowing this way and that and her arms clinging round his neck and him saying "There there there! Now let me go Peggy." And by that time it was plain that what the Major had been so accommodating as to say he would not object to happening in the house, would happen in it, and I told her as much when he was gone while I comforted her

with my arm up the staircase, for I says "You will soon have others to keep up for my pretty and you must think of that."

His letter never came when it ought to have come and what she went through morning after morning when the postman brought none for her the very postman himself compassionated when she ran down to the door, and yet we cannot wonder at its being calculated to blunt the feelings to have all the trouble of other people's letters and none of the pleasure and doing it oftener in the mud and mizzle than not and at a rate of wages more resembling Little Britain than Great. But at last one morning when she was too poorly to come running down stairs he says to me with a pleasant look in his face that made me next to love the man in his uniform coat though he was dripping wet "I have taken you first in the street this morning Mrs. Lirriper, for here's the one for Mrs. Edson." I went up to her bedroom with it fast as ever I could go, and she sat up in bed when she saw it and kissed it and tore it open and then a blank stare came upon her. "It's very short!" she says lifting her large eyes to my face. "Oh Mrs. Lirriper it's very short!" I says "My dear Mrs. Edson no doubt that's because your husband hadn't time to write more just at that time." "No doubt, no doubt," says she, and puts her two hands on her face and turns round in her bed.

I shut her softly in and I crept down stairs and I tapped at the Major's door, and when the Major having his thin slices of bacon in his own Dutch oven saw me he come out of his chair and put me down on the sofa. "Hush!" says he, "I see something's the matter. Don't speak—take time." I says "O Major I'm afraid there's cruel work up-stairs." "Yes yes" says he "I had begun to be afraid of it—take time." And then in opposition to his own words he rages out frightfully, and says "I shall never forgive myself Madam, that I, Jemmy Jackman, didn't see it all that morning—didn't go straight up-stairs when my boot sponge was in my hand—didn't force it down his throat—and choke him dead with it on the spot!"

The Major and me agreed when we came to ourselves that just at present we could do no more than take on to suspect nothing and use our best endeavors to keep that poor young creature quiet, and what I ever should have done without the Major when it got about among the organ-men that quiet was our object is unknown, for he made lion and tiger war upon them to that degree that without seeing it I could not have believed it was in any gentleman to have such a power of bursting out with fire-irons walking-sticks water-jugs coals potatoes off his table the very hat off his head, and at the same time so furious in foreign language that they would stand with their handles half turned fixed like the. Sleeping Ugly—for I cannot say Beauty.

Ever to see the postman come near the house now gave me such a fear that it was a reprieve when he went by, but in about another ten days or a fortnight he says again "Here's one for Mrs. Edsom.—Is she pretty well?" "She is pretty well postman, but not well enough to rise so early as she used" which was so far gospel truth.

I carried the letter in to the Major at his breakfast and I says tottering "Major I have not the courage to take it up to her."

"It's an ill-looking villain of a letter," says the Major.

"I have not the courage Major" I says again in a tremble "to take it up to her."

After seeming lost in consideration for some moments the Major says, raising his head as if something new and useful had occurred to his mind "Mrs. Lirriper, I shall never forgive myself that I, Jemmy Jackman, didn't go straight upstairs that morning when my boot sponge was in my hand—and force it down his throat—and choke him dead with it."

"Major" I says a little hasty "you didn't do it which is a blessing, for it would have done no good and I think your sponge was better employed on your own honourable boots."

So we got to be rational, and planned that I should tap at her bedroom door and lay the letter on the mat outside and wait on the upper landing for what might happen, and never was gunpowder cannon-balls or shells or rockets more dreaded than that dreadful letter was by me as I took it to the second floor.

A terrible loud scream sounded through the house the minute after she had opened it, and I found her on the floor lying as if her life was gone. My dear I never looked at the face of the letter which was lying open by her, for there was no occasion.

Everything I needed to bring her round the Major brought up with his own hands, besides running out to the chemist's for what was not in the house and likewise having the fiercest of all his many skirmishes with a musical instrument representing a ball-room I do not know in what particular country and company waltzing in and out at folding-doors with rolling eyes When after a long time I saw her coming to, I slipped on the landing till I heard her cry, and then I went in and says cheerily "Mrs. Edson you're not well my dear and it's not to be wondered at," as if I had not been in before.—

Whether she believed or disbelieved I cannot say and it would signify nothing if I could, but I stayed by her for hours and then she God ever blesses me! and says she will try to rest for her head is bad.

"Major," I whispers, looking in at the parlours, "I beg and pray of you don't go out."

The Major whispers "Madam, trust me I will do no such a thing. How is she?"

I says "Major the good Lord above us only knows what burns and rages in her poor mind. I left her sitting at her window. I am going to sit at mine."

It came on afternoon and it came on evening. Norfolk is a delightful street to lodge in—provided you don't go lower down—but of a summer evening when the dust and waste paper lie in it and stray children play in it and a kind of a gritty calm and bake settles on it and a peal of church-bells is practising in the neighborhood it is a trifle dull, and never have I seen it since at such a time and never shall I see it evermore at such a time without seeing the dull June evening when that forlorn young creature sat at her open corner window on the second and me at my open corner window (the other corner) on the third. Something merciful, something wiser and better far than my own self, had moved me while it was yet light to sit in my bonnet and shawl, and as the shadows fell and the tide rose I could sometimes—when I put out my head and looked at her window below—see that she leaned out a little looking down the street. It was just settling dark when I saw her in the street.

So fearful of losing sight of her that it almost stops my breath while I tell it, I went down stairs faster than I ever moved in all my life and only tapped with my hand at the Major's door in passing it and slipped out. She was gone already. I made the same speed down the street and when I came to the corner of Howard-street I saw that she had turned it and was there plain before me going towards the west. O with what a thankful heart I saw her going along!

She was quite unacquainted with London and had very seldom been out for more than an airing in our own street where she knew two or three little children belonging to neighbours and had sometimes stood among them at the end of the street looking at the water. She must be going at hazards I knew, still she kept the by-streets quite correctly as long as they would serve her, and then turned up into the Strand. But at every corner I could see her head turned one way, and that way was always the river way.

It may have been only the darkness and quiet of the Adelphi that caused her to strike into it.

but she struck into it much us readily as if she had set out to go there, which perhaps was the case. She went straight down to the Terrace and along it and looked over the iron rail, and I often woke afterwards in my own bed with the horror of seeing her doing it. The desertion of the wharf below and the flowing of the high water'there seemed to settle her purpose. She looked about us if to make out the way down, and she struck out the right way or the wrong way—I don't know which, for I don't know the place before or since—and I followed her the way she went.

It was noticeable that all this time she never once looked back. But there was now a great change in the manner of her going, and instead of going at a steady quick walk with her arms folded before her,—among the dark dismal arches she went in a wild way with her arms opened wide, as if they were wings and she was flying to her death.

We were on the wharf and she stopped. I stopped. I saw her hands at her bonnet-strings, and I rushed between her and the brink and took her round the waist with both my arms. She might have drowned me, I felt then, but she could never have got quit of me.

Down to that moment my mind had been all in a maze and not half an idea had I had in it what I should say to her, but the instant I touched her it came to me like magic and I had my natural voice and my senses and even almost my breath.

"Mrs. Edson!" I says "My dear! Take care. How ever did you lose your way and stumble on a dangerous place like this? Why you must have come here by the most perplexing streets in all London. No wonder you are lost, I am sure. And this place too! Why I thought nobody ever got here, except me to order my coals and the Major in the parlours to smoke his cigar!"—for I saw that blessed man close by, pretending to it.

"Hah—Hah—Hum!" coughs the Major.

"And good gracious me" I says, "why here he is!"

"Halloa! who goes there!" says the Major in a military manner.

"Well!" I says, "if this don't beat everything! Don't you know us Major Jackman?"

"Halloa!" says the Major. "Who calls on Jemmy Jackman?" (and more out of breath he was, and did it less like-life, than I should have expected.

"Why here's Mrs. Edson Major" I says, "strolling out to cool her poor head which has been very bad, has missed her way and got lost, and Goodness knows where she might have got

to but for me coming here to drop an order into my coal merchant's letter-box and you coming here to smoke your cigar!—And you really are not well enough my dear" I says to her "to be half so far from home without me.—And your arm will be very acceptable I am sure Major" I says to him "and I know she may lean upon it as heavy as she likes." And now we had both got her—thanks be Above!—one on each side.

She was all in a cold shiver and she so continued till I laid her on her own bed, and up to the early morning she held me by the hand and moaned and moaned "O wicked, wicked, wicked!" But when at last I made believe to droop my head and be overpowered with a dead sleep, I heard that poor young creature give such touching and such humble thanks for being preserved from taking her own life in her madness that I thought I should have cried my eyes out on the counterpane and I knew she was safe.

Being well enough to do and able to afford it, me and the Major laid our little plan next day while she was asleep worn out, and so I says to her as soon as I could do it nicely:

"Mrs. Edson my dear, when Mr. Edson paid me the rent for these further six months——"

She gave a start and I felt her large eyes look at me, but I went on with it and with my. needlework.

"——I can't say that I am quite sure I dated the receipt right. Could you let me look at it ?"

She laid her frozen cold hand upon mine and she looked through me when I was forced to look up from my needlework; but I had taken the precaution of having on my spectacles.

"I have no receipt" says she.

"Ah! Then he has got it" I says in a careless way. "It's of no great consequence. A receipt's a receipt."

From that time she always had hold of my hand when I could spare it which was generally only when I read to her, for of course she and me had our bits of needlework to plod at and neither of us was very handy at those little things, though I am still rather proud of my share in them too considering. And though she took to all I read to her, I used to fancy that next to what was taught upon the Mount she took most of all to His young life and to how his mother was proud of him and treasured His sayings. in her heart. She had a grateful look in her eyes that never never never will be out of mine until they are closed in my last sleep, and when I chanced to look at her without thinking of it I would always meet that look, and she would often offer me her trembling lips to kiss, much more like a little affectionate half-broken-hearted child than ever I can imagine any grown person.

One time the trembling of this poor lip was so strong and her tears ran down so fast that I thought she was going to tell me all her woe, so I takes her two hands in mine and I says:

"No my dear not now, you had best not try it now. Wait for better times when you have got over this and are strong, and then you shall tell me whatever you will. Shall it be agreed?"

With our hands still joined she nodded her head many times, and she lifted my hands and put them to her lips and to her bosom.

"Only one word now my dear" I says. "Is there any one?"

She looked inquiringly "Any one?"

"That I can go to!"

She shook her head.

"No one that I can bring!"

She shook her head.

"No one is wanted by me my dear. Now that may be considered past and gone."

Not much more than a week afterwards—for this was far in the time of our being so together—I was bending over at her bedside with my ear down to her lips, by turns listening for her breath and looking for a sign of life in her face. At last it came in a solemn way—not in a flash but like a kind of palefaint light brought very slow to the face.

She said something to me that had no sound in it, but I saw she asked me:

"Is this death?"

And I says "Poor dear poor dear, I think it is."

Knowing somehow that she wanted me to move her weak right hand, I took it and laid it on her breast and then folded her other hand upon it, and she prayed a good good prayer and I join in it poor me though there were no words spoke. Then I brought the baby in its wrappers from where it lay, and I says:

"My dear this is sent to a childless old woman. This is for me to take care of."

The trembling lips was put up towards my face for the last time, and I dearly kissed it.

"Yes my dear" I says. "Please God! me and the Major."

I don't know how to tell it right, but I saw her soul brighten and leap up, and get free and fly away in the grateful look.

*   *   *   *   *   *

So this is the why and wherefore of its coming to pass my dear that we called him Jemmy, being after the Major his own godfather with Lirriper for a surname being after myself, and never was a dear child such a brightening thing in a Lodgings or such a playmate to his grandmother as Jemmy to this house and me, and always good and minding what he was told (upon the whole) and soothing for the temper and making everything

pleasanter except when he grew old enough to drop his cap down Wozenham's Airy and they wouldn't hand it up to him, and being worked into a state I put on my best bonnet and gloves and parasol with the child in my hand and I says "Miss Wozenham I little thought ever to have entered your house but unless my grandson's cap is instantly restored, the laws of this country regulating the property of the Subject shall at length decide betwixt yourself and me, cost what it may." With a sneer upon her face which did strike me I must say as being expressive of two keys but it may have been a mistake and if there is any doubt lest Miss Wozenham have the full benefit of it as is but right, she rang the bell and she says "Jane is there a street-child's old cap down our Airy?" "Miss Wozenham before your housemaid answers that question you must allow me to inform you to your face that my grandson is not a street-child and is not in the habit of wearing old caps. In fact" I says "Miss Wozenham I am fur' from sure that my grandson's cap may not be newer than your own" which was perfectly savage in me, her lace being the commonest machine-make washed and torn besides, but I have been put into a state to begin with fomented by impertinence. Miss Wozenham says red in the face "Jane you heard my question, is there any child's cap down our Airy?" "Yes Ma'am" says Jane "I think I did see some such rubbish a lying there." "Then" says Miss Wozenham "let these visitors out, and then throw up that worthless article out of my premises." But here the child who had been staring at Miss Wozenham with all his eyes and more, frowns down his little eyebrows purses up his little mouth puts his chubby legs far apart torns his little dimpled fists round and round slowly over one another like a little coffee-mill, and says to her "Oo impdent to mi Gran, me tut oor hi!" "Oh!" says Miss Wozenham looking down scornfully at the Mite "this is not a street-child is it not! Really!" I bursts out laughing and I says "Miss Wozenham if this an't a pretty sight to you I don't envy your feelings and I wish you good day. Jemmy come along with Gran." And I was still in the best of humours though his cap came flying up into the street as if it had been just turned on out of the water-plug, and I went home laughing all the way, all owing to that dear boy.

The miles and miles that me and the Major have travelled with Jemmy in the dusk between the lights are not to be calculated, Jemmy driving on the coach-box which is the Major's brass bound writing-desk on the table, me inside in the easy chair and the Major Guard up behind with a brown-paper horn doing it wonderful. I do assure you my dear that sometimes when I have taken a few winks in my place inside the coach and have come half awake by the flashing light of the fire and have heard that precious pet driving and the Major blowing up behind to have the change of horses ready when we got to the Inn, I have half believed we were on the old North Road that my poor Lirriper knew so well. Then to see that child and the Major both wrapped up getting down to warm their feet and going stamping about and having glasses of ale out of the paper match-boxes on the chimney pieces is to see the Major enjoing it fully as much as the child I am very sure, and its equal to any play when Coachee opens the coach-door to look in at me inside and say "Wery 'past that 'tage.—'Prightened old lady?"

But what my inexpressible feelings were when we lost that child can only be compared to the Major's which were not a shade better, through his straying out at five years old and eleven o'clock in the forenoon and never heard of by word or sign or deed till half-past nine at night, when the Major had gone to the Editor of the Times newspaper to put in an advertisement, which came out next day four and twenty hours after he was found, and which I mean always carefully to keep in my lavender drawer as the first printed account of him. The more the day gone on, the more I got distracted and the Major too and both of us made worse by the composed ways of the police though very civil and obliging and what I must call their obstinacy in not entertaining the idea that he was stolen. "We mostly find Mum" says the sergeant who came round to comfort me, which he didn't at all and he had been one of the private constables in Caroline's time to which he referred in his opening words when he said "Don't give way to uneasiness in your mind Mum, it'll all come as right as my nose did when I got the same barked by that young woman in your second floor"—says this sergeant "we mostly find Mum as people ain't over anxious to have what I may call second-hand children. You'll get him back Mum." "O but my dear good sir" I says clasping my hands and wringing them and clasping them again "he is such an uncommon child!" "Yes Mum" says the sergeant, "we mostly find that too Mum. The question is what his clothes were worth." "His clothes" I 'says "were not worth much sir for he had only got his playing-dress on, but the dear child!——" "All right Mum" says the sergeant. "You'll get him back Mum. And even if he'd had his best clothes on it wouldn't come to worse than his being found wrapped up in a cabbage-leaf, a shivering in a lane." His words pierced my heart like daggers

and daggers, and me and the Major ran in and out like wild things all day long till the Major returning from his interview with the Editor of the Times at night rushes into my little room hysterical and squeezes my hand and wipes his eyes and says "Joy joy—officer in plain clothes came up on the steps as I was letting myself in—compose your feelings—Jemmy's found." Consequently I fainted away and when I came to embrace the legs of the officer in plain clothes who seemed to be taking a kind of quiet inventory in his mind of the property in my little room with brown whiskers, and I says "Blessing on you sir where is the Darling!" and he says "In Kennington Station House." I was dropping at his feet Stone at the image of that Innocence in cells with murderers when he adds "He followed the Monkey." I says deeming it slang language "Oh sir explain for a loving grandmother what Monkey! He says "him in the spangled cap with the strap under the chin, as won't keep on—him as sweeps the crossings on a round table and don't want to draw his sabre more than he can help." Then I understood it all and most thankfully thanked him, and me and the Major and him drove over to Kennington and there we found our boy lying quite comfortable before a blazing fire, having sweetly played himself to sleep upon a small accordeon nothing like so big as a flat iron which they had been so kind as to lend him for the purpose and which it appeared had been stopped upon a very young person.

My dear, the system upon which the Major commenced, and as I may say perfected Jemmy's learning when he was so small that if the dear was on the other side of the table you had to look under it instead of over it to see him with his mother's own bright hair in beautiful curls, is a thing that ought to be known to the Throne and Lords and Commons, and then might obtain some promotion for the Major which he well deserves, and would be none the worse for (speaking between friends) L. S. D.-ically. When the Major undertook his learning, he says to me:

" I'm going Madam," he says, " to make our child a Calculating Boy."

" Major," I says, "you terrify me, and may do the pet a permanent injury you would never forgive yourself."

" Madam," says the Major, "next to my regret that when I had my boot-sponge in my hand, I didn't choke that scoundrel with it—on the spot——"

" There ! For Gracious sake !" I interrupts, "let his conscience find him without sponges."

" ——I say next to that regret, Madam," says the Major, " would be the regret with which my breast," which he tapped, "would be surcharged if this fine mind was not early cultivated. But mark me, Madam," says the Major, holding up his forefinger, "cultivated on a principle that will make it a delight."

"Major," I says, "I will be candid with you, and tell you openly that if ever I find the dear child fall off in his appetite, I shall know it is his calculations, and shall put a stop to them at two minutes' notice. Or if I find them must ing to his head," says I, "or striking any ways cold to his stomach, or leading to anything approaching flubbiness in his legs, the result will be the same; but Major you are a clever man, and have seen much, and you love the child, and are his own godfather, and if you feel a confidence in trying try."

"Spoken, Madam," says the Major "like Emma Lirriper. All I have to ask, Madam, is, that you will leave my godson and myself to make a week or two's preparation for surprising you, and that you will give me leave to have up and down any small articles not actually in use that I may require from the kitchen."

"From the kitchen Major!" I says, half feeling as if he had a mind to cook the child.

"From the kitchen," says the Major, and smiles and swells, and at the same time looks taller.

So I passed my word and the Major and the dear boy were shut up together for half an hour at a time through a certain while, and never could I hear anything going on betwixt them but talking and laughing and Jemmy clapping his hands and screaming out numbers, so I says to myself, "it has not harmed him yet," nor could I on examining the dear find any signs of it anywhere about him which was likewise a great relief. At last one day Jemmy brings me a card in joke in the Major's neat writing "The Messrs. Jemmy Jackman" for we had given him the Major's other name too "request the honour of Mrs Lirriper's company at the Jackman Institution in the front parlour this evening at five, military time, to witness a few slight feats of elementary arithmetic." And if you'll believe me there in the front parlour at five punctual to the moment was the Major behind the Pembroke table with both leaves up and a lot of things from the kitchen tidily set out on old newspapers spread atop of it, and there was the Mite stood upon a chair with his rosy cheeks flushing and his eyes sparkling clusters of diamonds.

"Now Gran" says he, "oo tit down and don't oo touch ler poople"—for he saw with every one of those diamonds of his that I was going to give him a squeeze.

"Very well sir" I says "I am obedient in this good company I am sure." And I sits down in the easy-chair that was put for me, shaking my sides.

But picture my admiration when the Major going on almost as quick as if he was conjuring sets out all the articles he names, and says "Three saucepans, an Italian iron, a hand-bell, a toasting fork, a nutmeg-grater, four pot-lids, a spice-box, two egg-cups, and a chopping-board, how many?" and when that Mite instantly cries "Tifteen, tut down tive and carry ler 'toppin-board" and then claps his hands draws up his legs and dances on his chair!

My dear with the same astonishing ease and correctness him and the Major added up the tables chairs and sofy, the picters fender and fireirons their own selves me and the cat and the eyes in Miss Wozenham's head, and whenever the sum was done Young Roses and Diamonds claps his hands and draws up his legs and dances on his chair.

The pride of the Major! ("Here's a mind Ma'am!" he says to me behind his hand.)

Then he says aloud, "We now come to the next elementary rule: which is called——"

"Umtraction!" cries Jemmy.

"Right," says the Major. "We have here a toasting-fork, a potato in its natural state, two pot-lids, one egg-cup, a wooden spoon, and two skewers, from which it is necessary for commercial purposes to subtract a sprat-gridiron, a small pickle-jar, two lemons, one pepper-castor, a black beetle-trap, and a knob of the dresser-drawer—what remains?"

"Toatin-fork!" cries Jemmy.

"In numbers how many?" says the Major.

"One!" cries Jemmy.

("Here's a boy, Ma'am!" says the Major to me, behind his hand.)

Then the Major goes on:

"We now approach the next elementary rule: which is entitled——"

"Tickleication!" cries Jemmy.

"Correct" says the Major.

But my dear to relate to you in detail the way in which they multiplied fourteen sticks of firewood by two bits of ginger and a larding-needle, or divided pretty well everything else there was on the table by the heater of the Italian iron and a chamber candlestick, and got a lemon over, would make my head spin round and round and round as it did at the time. So I says "if you'll excuse my addressing the chair Professor Jackman I think the period of the lecture has now arrived when it becomes necessary that I should take a good hug of this young scholar." Upon which Jemmy calls out from his station on the chair, "Gran oo open oor arms and me'll make a 'pring into 'em." So I opened my arms

tò him as I had opened my sorrowful heart when
his poor young mother lay a dying, and he had
his jump and we had a good long hug together,
and the Major prouder than any peacock says
to me behind his hand, "You need not let him
know it Madam" (which I certainly need not
for the Major was quite audible) "but he is a
boy!"

In this way Jemmy grew and grew and went
to day-school and continued under the Major
too, and in the summer we were as happy as the
days were long and in winter we were as happy
as the days were short and there seemed to rest
a Blessing on the Lodgings for they as good as
Let themselves and would have done it if there
had been twice the accommodation, when sore
and hard against my will I one day says to the
Major.

"Major you know what I am going to break
to you. Our boy must go to boarding-school."

It was a sad sight to see the Major's countenance drop, and I pitied the good soul with all
my heart.

"Yes Major" I says "though he is as popular
with the Lodgers as you are yourself and though
he is to you and me what only you and me
know, still it is in the course of things and Life
is made of partings, and we must part with our
Pet."

Bold as I spoke, I saw two Majors and half a
dozen fire-places, and when the poor Major put
one of his neat bright-varnished boots upon the
fender and his elbow on his knee and his head
upon his hand and rocked himself a little to and
fro, I was dreadfully cut up.

"But" says I clearing my throat, "you have
so well prepared him Major—he has had such a
Tutor in you—that he will have none of the first
drudgery to go through. And he is so clever
besides that he'll soon make his way to the front
rank."

"He is a boy" says the Major—having sniffed
—"that has not his like on the face of the
earth."

"True as you say Major, and it is not for us
merely for our own sakes to do anything to keep
him back from being a credit and an ornament
wherever he goes and perhaps even rising to be
a great man, is it Major? He will have all my
little savings when my work is done (being all
the world to me) and we must try to make him a
wise man and a good man, mustn't we Major?"

"Madam" says the Major rising, "Jemmy
Jackman is becoming an older file than I was
aware of, and you put him to shame. You are
thoroughly right Madam. You are simply and
undeniably right.—And if you'll excuse me, I'll
take a walk."

So the Major being gone out and Jemmy being at home, I got the child into my little room
here and I stood him by my chair and I took
his mother's own curls in my hand and I spoke
to him loving and serious. And when I had re-
minded the darling how that he was now in his
tenth year and when I had said to him about his
getting on in life pretty much what I had said to
the Major I broke to him how that we must have
this same parting, and there I was forced to stop
for there I saw of a sudden the well remembered
lip with its tremble, and it so brought back that
time! But with the spirit that was in him he
controlled it soon and he says gravely nodding
through his tears, "I understand Gran—I know
it must be, Gran—go on Gran, don't be afraid of
me." And when I had said all that ever I could
think of, he turned his bright steady face to mine
and he says just a little broken here and there
"You shall see Gran that I can be a man and that
I can do anything that is grateful and loving to
you—and if I do'nt grow up to be what you would
like to have me—I hope it will be—because I
shall die." And with that he sat down by me,
and I went on to tell him of the school of which
I had excellent recommendations and where it
was and how many scholars and what games
they played as I had heard and what length of
holidays, to all of which he listened bright and
clear. And so it came that at last he says "And
now dear Gran let me kneel down here where I
have been used to say my prayers and let me fold
my face for just a minute in your gown and let
me cry, for you have been more than father—
more than mother—more than brothers sisters
friends—to me!" And so he did cry and I too
and we were both much the better for it.

From that time forth he was true to his word
and ever blithe and ready, and even when me
and the Major took him down into Lincolnshire
he was far the gayest of the party though for
sure and certain he might easily have been that,
but he really was and put life into us only when
it came to the last Good-by, he says with a wist-
ful look "You wouldn't have me not really sorry
would you Gran?" and when I says "No dear,
Lord forbid!" he says "I am glad of that!" and
ran in out of sight.

But now that the child was gone out of the
Lodgings the Major fell into a regularly moping
state. It was taken notice of by all the Lodgers
that the Major moped. He hadn't even the
same air of being rather tall that he used to
have, and if he varnished his boots with a single
gleam of interest it was as much as he did.

One evening the Major came into my little
room to take a cup of tea and a morsel of buttered
toast and to read Jemmy's newest letter which

had arrived that afternoon (by the very same postman more than middle-aged upon the Beat now), and the letter raising him up a little I says to the Major:

" Major you mustn't get into a moping way."

The Major shook his head. "Jemmy Jackman ,Madam," he says with a deep sigh, "is an elder file than I thought him."

" Moping is not the way to grow younger, Major."

"My dear Madam," says the Major, "is there any way of growing younger ?"

Feeling that the Major was getting rather the best of that point, I made a diversion to another.

"Thirteen years! Thirteen years! Many Lodgers have come and gone, in the thirteen years that you have lived in the parlours Major."

"Hah!" says the Major warming. "Many, Madam, many."

"And I should say you have been familiar with them all ?"

"As a rule (with its exceptions like all rules) my dear Madam," says the Major, "they have honoured me with their acquaintance, and not unfrequently with their confidence."

Watching the Major as he drooped his white head and stroked his black moustachios and moped again, a thought which I think must have been going about looking for an owner somewhere dropped into my old noddle if you will excuse the expression.

" The walls of my Lodgings" I says in a casual way—for my dear it is of no use going straight at a man who mopes—"might have something to tell, if they could tell it."

The Major neither moved nor said anything but I saw he was attending with his shoulders my dear—attending with his shoulders to what I said. 'In fact I saw that his shoulders were struck by it.

"The dear boy was always fond of story-books" I went on, like as if I was talking to myself.— "I am sure this house—his own home—might write a story or two for his reading one day or another."

The Major's shoulders gave a dip and a curve and his head came up in his shirt collar. The Major's head came up in his shirt-collar as I hadn't seen it come up since Jemmy went to school.

"It is unquestionable that in intervals of cribbage and a friendly rubber, my dear Madam," says the Major, "and also over what used to be called in my young times—in the salad days of Jemmy Jackman—the social glass, I have exchanged many a reminiscence with your Lodgers."

My remark was—I confess I made it with the deepest and artfullest of intentions—"I wish our dear boy had heard them !"

"Are you serious Madam ?" asked the Major starting and turning full round.

" Why not Major ?"

"Madam" says the Major, turning up one of his cuffs, "they shall be written for him."

"Ah ! Now you speak" I says giving my hands a pleased clap. " Now you are in a way out of moping Major."

" Between this and my holidays—I mean the dear boy's"—says the Major turning up his other cuff, "a good deal may be done towards it."

"Major you are a clever man and you have seen much and not a doubt of it."

"I'll begin," says the Major, looking as tall as ever he did, "to-morrow."

My dear the Major was another man in three days and he was himself again in a week and he wrote and wrote and wrote with his pen scratching like rats behind the wainscot, and whether he had many grounds to go upon or whether he did at all romance I cannot tell you, but what he has written is in the left-hand glass closet of the little book-case close behind you, and if you'll put your hand in you'll find it come out heavy in lumps sewn together and being beautifully plain and unknown Greek and Hebrew to myself and me quite wakeful, I shall take it as a favour if you'll read out loud and read on.

———◆◆◆———

II.

HOW THE FIRST FLOOR WENT TO CROWLEY CASTLE.

I HAVE come back to London, Major, possessed by a family-story that I have picked up in the country. While I was out of town, I visited the ruins of the great old Norman castle of Sir Mark Crowley, the last baronet of his name, who had been dead nearly a hundred years. I stayed in the village near the castle, and thence I bring back some of the particulars of the tale I am going to tell you, derived from old inhabitants who heard them from their fathers ;—no longer ago.

We drove from our little sea-bathing place, in Sussex, to see the massive ruins of Crowley Castle, which is the show-excursion of Merton. We had to alight at a field gate; the road further on being too bad for the slightly-built carriage, or the poor tired Merton horse ; and we walked for about a quarter of a mile through uneven ground, which had once been an Italian garden ; and then we came to a bridge over a dry moat, and went over the groove of a portcullis that had once closed the massive entrance, into an empty space surrounded by thick walls, draperied with ivy, unroofed, and open to the sky. We could judge of the beautiful tracery that had been in the windows, by the remains of the stonework here and there ; and an old man—"ever so old," he called himself when we inquired his exact age—who scrambled and stumbled out of some lair in the least devastated part of the ruins at our approach, and who established himself as our guide, showed us a scrap of glass yet lingering in what was the window of the great drawing-room not above seventy years ago. After he had done his duty, he hobbled with us to the neighbouring church, where the knightly Crowleys lie buried : some commemorated by ancient brasses, some by altar-tombs, some by fine Latin epitaphs, bestowing upon them every virtue under the sun. He had to take the church-key back to the adjoining parsonage at the entrance of the long straggling street which forms the village of Crowley. The castle and the church were on the summit of a hill, from which we could see the distant line of sea beyond the misty marshes. The village fell away from the church and parsonage, down the hill. The aspect of the place was little, if at all changed from its aspect in the year 1772.

But I must begin a little earlier. From one of the Latin epitaphs I learnt that Amelia Lady Crowley died in 1756, deeply regretted by her loving husband, Sir Mark. He never married again, though his wife had left him no heir to his name or his estate—only a little tiny girl—Theresa Crowley. This child would inherit her mother's fortune, and all that Sir Mark was free to leave ; but this little was not much ; the castle and all the lands going to his sister's son, Marmaduke, or as he was usually called Duke, Brownlow. Duke's parents were dead, and his uncle was his guardian, and his guardian's house was his home. The lad was some seven or eight years older than his cousin ; and probably Sir Mark thought it not unlikely that his daughter and his heir might make a match. Theresa's mother had had some foreign blood in her, and had been brought up in France—not so far away but that its shores might be seen by any one who chose to take an easy day's ride from Crowley Castle for the purpose.

Lady Crowley had been a delicate elegant creature, but no great beauty, judging from all accounts ; Sir Mark's family were famous for their good looks ; Theresa, an unusually lucky child, inherited the outward graces of both her parents. A portrait which I saw of her, degraded to a station over the parlor chimney-piece in the village inn, showed me black hair, soft yet arch grey eyes with brows and lashes of the same tint of her hair, a full pretty passionate mouth,

and a round slender throat. She was a wilful creature, and her father's indulgence made her more wayward. She had a nurse, too, a French bonne, whose mother had been about my lady from her youth, who had followed my lady to England, and who had died there. Victorine had been in attendance on the young Theresa from her earliest infancy, and almost took the place of a parent in power and affection—in power, as to ordering and arranging almost what she liked, concerning the child's management—in love, because they speak to this day of the black year when virulent small-pox was rife in Crowley, and when, Sir Mark being far away on some diplomatic mission—in Vienna, I fancy—Victorine shut herself up with Miss Theresa, when the child was taken ill with the disease, and nursed her night and day. She only succumbed to the dreadful illness when all danger to the child was over. Theresa came out of it with unblemished beauty ; Victorine barely escaped with life, and was disfigured for life.

This disfigurement put a stop to much unfounded scandal which had been afloat respecting the French servant's great influence over Sir Mark. He was, in fact, an easy and indolent man, rarely excited to any vehemence of emotion, and who felt it to be a point of honour to carry out his dead wife's wish that Victorine should never leave Theresa, and that the management of the child should be confided to her. Only once had their been a struggle for power between Sir Mark and the bonne, and then she had won the victory. And no wonder, if the old butler's account were true ; for he had gone into the room unawares, and had found Sir Mark and Victorine at high words ; and he said that Victorine was white with rage, that her eyes were blazing with passionate fire, that her voice was low and her words were few, but that, although she spoke in French, and he the butler only knew his native English, he would rather have been sworn at by a drunken grenadier with a sword in his hand, than have those words of Victorine's addressed to him.

Even the choice of Theresa's masters was left to Victorine. A little reference was occasionally made to Madam Hawtrey, the parson's wife, and a distant relation of Sir Mark's, but, seeing that, if Victorine so chose to order it, Madam Hawtrey's own little daughter Bessy would have been deprived of the advantages resulting from gratuitous companionship in all Theresa's lessons, she was careful how she opposed or made an enemy of Mademoiselle Victorine. Bessy was a gentle quiet child, and grew up to be a sensible sweet-tempered girl, with a very fair share of English beauty ; fresh complexion, brown-eyed, round-faced, with a stiff though well-made figure, as different as possible from Theresa's slight lithe graceful form. Duke was a young man to these two maidens, while they to him were little more than children. Of course he admired his cousin Theresa the most—who would not?—but he was establishing his first principles of morality for himself, and her conduct towards Bessy sometimes jarred against his ideas of right. One day, after she had been tyrannising over the self-contained and patient Bessy so as to make the latter cry—and both the amount of the tyranny and the crying were unusual circumstances, for Theresa was of a generous nature when not put out of the way—Duke spoke to his cousin:

"Theresa! you had no right to blame Bessy as you did. It was as much your fault as hers. You were as much bound to remember Mr. Dawson's directions about the sums you were to do for him, as she was."

The girl opened her great grey eyes with surprise. She to blame!

"What does Bessy come to the castle for, I wonder? They pay nothing—we pay all. The least she can do is to remember for me what we are told. I shan't trouble myself with attending to Mr. Dawson's directions; and if Bessy does not like to do so, she can stay away. She already knows enough to earn her bread as a maid: which I suppose is what she'll have to come to."

The moment Theresa had said this, she could have bitten her tongue out for the meanness and rancour of the speech. She saw pain and disappointment clearly expressed on Duke's face; and in another moment her impulses would have carried her to the opposite extreme, and she would have spoken out her self-reproach. But Duke thought it his duty to remonstrate with her, and to read her a homily, which, however true and just, weakened the effect of the look of distress on his face. Her wits were called into play to refute his arguments; her head rather than her heart took the prominent part in the controversy; and it ended unsatisfactorily to both; he, going away with dismal though unspoken prognostics touching what she would become as a woman if she were so supercilious and unfeeling as a girl; she, the moment his back was turned, throwing herself on the floor and sobbing as if her heart would break. Victorine heard her darling's passionate sobs, and came in.

"What hast thou, my angel? Who has been vexing thee—tell me, my cherished?"

She tried to raise the girl, but Theresa would not be raised; neither would she speak till she chose, in spite of Victorine's entreaties. When she chose, she lifted herself up, still sitting on the floor, and putting her tangled hair off her flushed tear-stained face, said:

"Never mind, it was only something Duke said; I don't care for it now." And refusing Victorine's aid, she got up, and stood thoughtfully looking out of the window.

"That Duke!" exclaimed Victorine. "What business has that Mr. Duke to go vex my darling? He is not your husband yet, that he should scold you, or that you should mind what he says."

Theresa listened and gained a new idea; but she gave no outward sign of attention, or of her now hearing for the first time how that she was supposed to be intended for her cousin's wife.—She made no reply to Victorine's caresses and speeches; one might almost say she shook her off. As soon as she was left to herself, she took her hat, and going out alone, as she was wont, in the pleasure-grounds, she went down the terrace steps, crossed the bowling green, and opened a little wicket-gate which led into the garden of the parsonage. There, were Bessy and her mother, gathering fruit. It was Bessy whom Theresa sought; for there was something in Madam Hawtrey's silky manner that was always rather repugnant to her. However she was not going to shrink from her resolution because Madam Hawtrey was there. So she went up to the startled Bessy, and said to her, as if she was reciting a prepared speech: "Bessy, I behaved very crossly to you; I had no business to have spoken to you as I did."—"Will you forgive me?" was the pre-determined end of this confession; but somehow, when it came to that, she could not say it with Madam Hawtrey standing by, ready to smile and to courtesy as soon as she could catch Theresa's eye. There was no need to ask forgiveness though; for Bessy had put down her half-filled basket, and came softly up to Theresa, stealing her brown soil-stained little hand into the young lady's soft, white one, and looking up at her with loving, brown eyes.

"I am so sorry, but I think it was the sums on page 108. I have been looking and looking, and I am almost sure."

Her exculpatory tone caught her mother's ear, although her words did not.

"I am sure, Miss Theresa, Bessy is so grateful for the privileges of learning with you! It is such an advantage to her! I often tell her, 'Take pattern by Miss Theresa, and do as she does, and try and speak as she does, and there'll not be a parson's daughter in all Sussex to compare with you.' Don't I, Bessy?"

Theresa shrugged her shoulders—a trick she had caught from Victorine—and, turning to Bessy asked her what she was going to do with those gooseberries she was gathering? And as Theresa spoke, she lazily picked the ripest out of the basket, and ate them.

"They are for a pudding," said Bessy. "As soon as we have gathered enough, I am going in to make it."

"I'll come and help you!" said Theresa eagerly. "I should so like to make a pudding. Our Monsieur Antoine never makes gooseberry puddings."

Duke came past the parsonage an hour or so afterwards: and, looking in by chance through the open casement windows of the kitchen, saw Theresa pinned up in a bib and apron, her arms all over flour, flourishing a rolling-pin, and laughing and chattering with Bessy similarly attired. Duke had spent his morning ostensibly in fishing, but in reality in weighing in his own mind what he could say or do to soften the obdurate heart of his cousin. And here it was, all inexplicably right, as if by some enchanter's wand!

The only conclusion Duke could come to was the same that many a wise (and foolish) man had come to before his day :

"Well ! Women are past my comprehension, that's all !"

When all this took place, Theresa was about fifteen ; Bessy was perhaps six months older ; Duke was just leaving Oxford. His uncle, Sir Mark, was excessively fond of him ; yes! and proud, too, for he had distinguished himself at college, and every one spoke well of him. And he, for his part, loved Sir Mark, and, unspoiled by the fame and reputation he had gained at Christ Church, paid respectful deference to Sir Mark's opinions.

As Theresa grew older, her father supposed that he played his cards well in singing Duke's praises on every possible occasion. She tossed her head, and said nothing. Thanks to Victorine's revelations, she understood the tendency of her father's speeches. She intended to make her own choice of a husband when the time came ; and it might be Duke, or it might be some one else. When Duke did not lecture or prose, but was sitting his horse so splendidly at the meet, before the huntsman gave the blast, "Found ;" when Duke was holding his own discourse with other men ; when Duke gave her a short sharp word of command on any occasion ; then she decided that she would marry him, and no one else. But when he found fault, or stumbled about awkwardly in a minuet, or talked moralities against duelling, then she was sure that Duke should never become her husband. . She wondered if he knew about it ; if any one had told him, as Victorine had told her ; if her father had revealed his thoughts and wishes to his nephew, as plainly as he had done to his daughter? This last query

made her cheeks burn ; and, on the days when the suspicion had been brought by chance prominently before her mind, she was especially rude and disagreeable to Duke.

He was to go abroad on the grand tour of Europe, to which young men of fortune usually devoted three years. He was to have a tutor, because all young men of his rank had tutors ; else he was quite wise enough, and steady enough, to have done without one, and probably knew a good deal more about what was best to be observed in the countries they were going to visit, than Mr. Roberts, his appointed bear-leader. He was to come back full of historical and political knowledge, speaking French and Italian like a native, and having a smattering of barbarous German, and he was to enter the House as a county member, if possible—as a borough member at the worst ; and was to make a great success ; and then, as every one understood, he was to marry his cousin Theresa.

He spoke to her father about it, before starting on his travels. It was after dinner in Crowley Castle. Sir Mark and Duke sat alone, each pensive at the thought of the coming parting.

"Theresa is but young," said Duke, breaking into speech after a long silence, "but if you have no objection, uncle, I should like to speak to her before I leave England, about my—my hopes."

Sir Mark played with his glass, poured out some more wine, drank it off at a draught, and then replied :

"No, Duke, no. Leave her in peace with me. I have looked forward to having her for my companion through these three years ; they'll soon pass away" (to age, but not to youth), "and I should like to have her undivided heart till you come back. No, Duke ! Three years will soon pass away, and then we'll have a royal wedding."

Duke sighed, but said no more. The next day was the last. He wanted Theresa to go with him to take leave of the Hawtrey's at the parsonage, and of the villagers ; but she was wilful, and would not. He remembered, years afterwards, how Bessy's gentle, peaceful manner had struck him as contrasted with Theresa's, on that last day. Both girls regretted his departure. He had been so uniformly gentle and thoughtful in his behaviour to Bessy, that, without any idea of love, she felt him to be her pattern of noble, chivalrous manhood ; the only person, except her father, who was steadily kind to her. She admired his sentiments, she esteemed his principles, she considered his long evolvement of his ideas as the truest eloquence. He had lent her books, he had directed her studies ; all the advice and information which Theresa had reject-ed had fallen to Bessy's lot, and she had received it thankfully.

Theresa burst into a passion of tears as soon as Duke and his suite were out of sight. She had refused the farewell kiss her father had told her to give him, but had waved her white hand-kerchief out of the great drawing-room window (that very window in which the old guide showed me the small piece of glass still lingering). But Duke had ridden away with slack rein and down-cast head, without looking back.

His absence was a great blank in Sir Mark's life. He had never sought London much as a place of residence; in former days he had been suspected of favouring the Stuarts; but nothing could be proved against him, and he had sub-sided into a very tolerably faithful subject of King George the Third. Still, a cold shoulder having been turned to him by the court party at one time, he had become prepossessed against the English capital. On the contrary, his wife's predilections and his own tendencies had always made Paris a very agreeable place of residence to him. To Paris he at length resorted again, when the blank in his life oppressed him; and from Paris, about two years after Duke's depar-ture, he returned after a short absence from home, and suddenly announced to his daughter and the household that he had taken an apart-ment in the Rue Louis le Grand for the coming winter, to which there was to be an immediate re-moval of his daughter, Victorine, and certain other personal attendants and servants.

Nothing could exceed Theresa's mad joy at this unexpected news. She sprang upon her father's neck and kissed him till she was tired —whatever he was. She ran to Victorine, and told her to guess what "heavenly bliss" was go-ing to befal them, dancing round the middle-aged woman until she, in her spoilt impatience, was becoming angry, when, kissing her, she told her, and ran off to the Parsonage, and thence to the church, bursting in upon morning prayers—for it was All Saints' Day, although she had for-gotten it—and filliping a scrap of paper on which she had hastily written, " We are going to Paris for the winter—all of us," rolled into a ball, from the castle pew to that of the parson. She saw Bessy redden as she caught it, put it into her pocket unread, and, after an apologetic glance at the curtained seat in which Theresa was, go on with her meek responses. Theresa went out by the private door in a momentary fit of passion. " Stupid, cold-blooded creature!" she said to herself. But that afternoon, Bessy came to the castle, so sorry—and so losing her own sorrow in sympathy with her friend's gladness, that There-

sa took her into favour again. The girls parted with promises of correspondence, and with some regret: the greatest on Bessy's side. Some grand promises of Paris fashion, and presents of dress, Theresa made in her patronizing way; but Bessy did not seem to care much for them—which was fortunate, for they were never ful-filled.

Sir Mark had an idea in his head of perfect-ing Theresa's accomplishments and manners by Parisian masters and Parisian society. English residents in Venice, Florence, Rome, wrote to their friends at home about Duke. They spoke of him as of what we should, at the present day, call a "rising young man." His praises ran so high, that Sir Mark began to fear lest his hand-some nephew, fêted by princes, courted by am-bassadors, made love to by lovely Italian ladies, might find Theresa too country-bred for his taste.

Thus had come about, the engaging of the splendid apartment in the Rue Louis le Grand. The street itself is narrow, and now-a-days we are apt to think the situation close; but in those days it was the height of fashion; for, the great arbiter of fashion, the Duc de Richelieu, lived there, and, to inhabit an apartment in that street, was in itself a mark of bon ton. Victorine seem-ed almost crazy with delight when they took pos-session of their new abode. "This dear Paris! This lovely France! And now I see my young lady, my darling, my angel, in a room suited to her beauty and her rank: such as my lady her mother would have planned for her, if she had lived. Any allusion to her dead mother always touched Theresa to the quick. She was in her bed, under the blue silk curtains of an alcove, when Victorine said this,—being too much fa-tigued after her journey to respond to Victorine's rhapsodies; but now she put out her little hand and gave Victorine's a pressure of gratitude and pleasure. Next day she wandered about the rooms and admired their splendour almost to Vic-torine's content. Her father, Sir Mark, found a handsome carriage and horses for his darling's use; and also found that not less necessary arti-cle—a married lady of rank who would take his girl under her wing. When all these prelimina-ry arrangements were made, who so wildly happy as Theresa! Her carriage was of the newest fashion, fit to vie with any on the Cours de la Reine, the then fashionable drive. The box at the Grand Opéra, and at the Français, which she shared with Madame la Duchesse de G., was the centre of observation; Victorine was in her best humour, Theresa's credit at her dressmaker's was unlimited, her indulgent father was charmed with all she did and said. She had masters, it is true;

but, to a rich and beautiful young lady, masters were wonderfully complaisant, and with them as with all the world, she did what she pleased. Of Parisian society, she had enough, and more than enough. The duchess went everywhere, and Theresa went too. So did a certain Count de la Grange: some relation or connexion of the duchess: handsome, with a south of France handsomeness: with delicate features, marred by an over-softness of expression, from which (so men said) the tiger was occasionally seen to peep forth. But, for elegance of dress and demeanour, he had not his fellow in Paris—which of course meant, not in the world.

Sir Mark heard rumours of this man's conduct, which were not pleasing to him; but when he accompanied his daughter into society, the count was only as deferential as it became a gentleman to be to so much beauty and grace. When Theresa was taken out by the duchess to the opera, to balls, to petits soupers, without her father, then the count was more than deferential; he was adoring. It was a little intoxicating for a girl brought up in the solitude of an English village, to have so many worshippers at her feet all at once, in the great city; and the inbred coquetry of her nature came out, adding to her outward grace, if taking away from the purity and dignity of her character. It was Victorine's delight to send her darling out arrayed for conquest; her hair delicately powdered, and scented with maréchale; her little "mouches" put on with skill; the tiny half-moon patch, to lengthen the already almond-shaped eye; the minute star to give the effect of a dimple at the corner of her scarlet lips; the silver gauze looped up over the petticoat of blue brocade, distended over a hoop, much as gowns are worn in our days; the coral ornaments of her silver dress, matching with the tint of the high heels to her shoes. And, at night, Victorine was never tired of listening and questioning; of triumphing in Theresa's triumphs; of invariably reminding her that she was bound to marry her absent cousin, and return to the half-feudal estate of the old castle in Sussex.

Still, even now, if Duke had returned from Italy, all might have gone well; but when Sir Mark, alarmed by the various proposals he received for Theresa's hand from needy French noblemen, and by the admiration she was exciting everywhere, wrote to Duke, and urged him to join them in Paris on his return from his travels, Duke answered that three months were yet unexpired of the time allotted for the grand tour; and that he was anxious to avail himself of that interval to see something of Spain. Sir Mark read this letter aloud to Theresa, with many expressions of annoyance as he read. Theresa

merely said, "Of course, Duke does what he likes," and turned away to see some new lace brought for inspection. She heard her father sigh over a reperusal of Duke's letter, and she set her teeth in the anger she would not show in acts or words. That day the Count de Grange met with gentler treatment from her than he had done for many days—than he had done since her father's letter to Duke had been sent off to Genoa. As ill fortune would have it, Sir Mark had occasion to return to England at this time, and he, guileless himself, consigned Theresa and her maid Victorine, and her man Felix to the care of the duchess for three weeks. They were to reside at the Hotel de G. during this time. The duchess welcomed them in her most caressing manner, and showed Theresa the suite of rooms, with the little private staircase, appropriated to her use.

The Count de Grange was an habitual visitor at the house of his cousin the duchess, who was a gay Parisian, absorbed in her life of giddy dissipation. The count found means of influencing Victorine in his favor; not by money; so coarse a bribe would not have had no power over her; but by many presents, accompanied with sentimental letters, breathing devotion to her charge, and extremest appreciation of the faithful friend whom Theresa looked upon as a mother, and whom for this reason he, the count, revered and loved. Intermixed, were wily allusions to his great possessions in Provence, and to his ancient lineage:—the one mortgaged, the other disgraced. Victorine, whose right hand had forgotten its cunning in the length of her dreary vegetation at Crowley Castle, was deceived, and became a vehement advocate of the dissolute Adonis of the Paris saloons, in his suit to her darling.— When Sir Mark came back, he was dismayed and shocked beyond measure by finding the count and Theresa at his feet, entreating him to forgive their stolen marriage—a marriage which, though incomplete as to its legal forms, was yet too complete to be otherwise than sanctioned by Theresa's nearest friends. The duchess accused her cousin of perfidy and treason. Sir Mark said nothing. But his health failed from that time, and he sank into an old querulous grey-haired man.

There was some ado, I know not what, between Sir Mark and the count regarding the control and disposition of the fortune Theresa inherited from her mother. The count gained the victory, owing to the different nature of the French laws from the English; and this made Sir Mark abjure the country and the city he had loved so long. Henceforward, he swore, his foot should never touch French soil; if Theresa liked to come and see him at Crowley Castle, she should be as welcome as a daughter of the house ought to be, and ever should be; but her husband should never enter the gates of the house in Sir Mark's lifetime.

For some months he was out of humour with Duke, because of his tardy return from his tour and his delay in joining them in Paris: through which, so Sir Mark fancied, Theresa's marriage had been brought about. But—when Duke came home, depressed in spirits and submissive to his uncle, even under unjust blame—Sir Mark restored him to favour in the course of a summer's day, and henceforth added another injury to the debtor side of the count's reckoning.

Duke never told his uncle of the woful ill-report he had heard of the count in Paris, where he had found all the better part of the French nobility pitying the lovely English heiress who had been entrapped into a marriage with one of the most disreputable of their order, a gambler and a reprobate. He could not leave Paris without seeing Theresa, whom he believed to be as yet unacquainted with his arrival in the city, so he went to call upon her one evening. She was sitting alone, splendidly dressed, ravishingly beautiful; she made a step forward to meet him, hardly heeding the announcement of his name; for she had recognized a man's tread, and fancied it was her husband, coming to accompany her to some grand reception. Duke saw the quick change from hope to disappointment on her mobile face, and she spoke out at once her reason. "Adolphe promised to come and fetch me; the princess receives to-night. I hardly expected a visit from you, cousin Duke," recovering herself into a pretty proud reserve. "It is a fortnight, I think, since I heard you were in Paris. I had given up all expectation of the honour of a visit from you!"

Duke felt that, as she had heard of his being there, it would be awkward to make excuses which both she and he must know to be false; or explanations the very truth of which would be offensive to the loving, trusting, deceived wife. So he turned the conversation to his travels, his heart aching for her all the time, as he noticed her wandering attention when she heard any passing sound. Ten, eleven, twelve o'clock; he would not leave her. He thought his presence was a comfort and a pleasure to her. But when one o'clock struck, she said some unexpected business must have detained her husband, and she was glad of it, as she had all along felt too much tired to go out: and besides, the happy consequence of her husband's detention had been that long talk with Duke.

He did not see her again after this police dismissal, nor did he see her husband at all — Whether through ill chance, or carefully disguis-

ed purpose, it did so happen that he called several times, he wrote several notes requesting an appointment when he might come with the certainty of finding the count and countess at home, in order to wish them farewell before setting out for England. All in vain. But he said nothing to Sir Mark of all this. He only tried to fill up the blank in the old man's life. He went between Sir Mark and the tenants, to whom he was unwilling to show himself unaccompanied by the beautiful daughter, who had so often been his companion in his walks and rides, before that ill-omened winter in Paris. He was thankful to have the power of returning the long kindness his uncle had shown him in childhood; thankful to be of use to him in his desertion; thankful to atone in some measure for his neglect of his uncle's wish that he should have made a hasty return to Paris.

But it was a little dull after the long excitement of travel, after associating with all that was most cultivated and seeing all that was most famous in Europe, to be shut up in that vast magnificent old castle, with Sir Mark for a perpetual companion—Sir Mark, and no other. The parsonage was near at hand, and occasionally Mr. Hawtrey came in to visit his parishioner in his trouble. But Sir Mark kept the clergyman at bay; he knew that his brother in age, his brother in circumstances, (for had not Mr. Hawtrey an only child and she a daughter?) was sympathizing with him in sorrow, and he was too proud to bear it; indeed, sometimes he was so rude to his old neighbour, that Duke would go next morning to the Parsonage, to soothe the smart.

And so—and so—gradually, imperceptibly, at last his heart was drawn to Bessy. Her mother angled, and angled skilfully; at first scarcely daring to hope; then remembering her own descent from the same stock as Duke, she drew herself up, and set to work with fresh skill and vigour. To be sure it was a dangerous game for a mother to play; for her daughter's happiness was staked on her success. How could simple, country-bred Bessy help being attracted to the courtly, handsome man, travelled and accomplished, good and gentle, whom she saw every day, and who treated her with the kind familiarity of a brother; while he was not a brother, but in some measure a disappointed man, as everybody knew? Bessy was a daisy of an English maiden; pure good to the heart's core and most hidden thought; sensible in all her accustomed daily ways, yet not so much without imagination as not to desire something beyond the narrow range of knowledge and experience in which her days had hitherto been passed. Add to this her pretty figure, a bright healthy complexion, lovely teeth, and quite enough of beauty in her features to have rendered her the belle of a country town, if her lot had been cast in such a place; and it is not to be wondered at, that, after she had been secretly in love with Duke with all her heart for nearly a year, almost worshipping him, he should discover that of all the women he had ever known—except perhaps the lost Theresa—Bessy Hawtrey had it in her power to make him the happiest of men.

Sir Mark grumbled a little; but now-a-days he grumbled at every thing, poor disappointed, all but childless, old man. As to the vicar he stood astonished and almost dismayed. "Have you thought enough about it, Mr. Duke?" the parson asked. "Young men are apt to do things in a hurry, that they repent at leisure. Bessy is a good girl, a good girl, God bless her; but she has not been brought up as your wife should have been: at least as folks will say your wife should have been. Though I may say for her she has a very pretty sprinkling of mathematics. I taught her myself, Mr. Duke?"

"May I go and ask her myself? I only want your permission," urged Duke.

"Ay, go! But perhaps you'd better ask Madam first. She will like to be told everything as soon as me."

But Duke did not care for Madam. He rushed through the open door of the Parsonage, into the homely sitting-rooms, and softly called for Bessy. When she came, he took her by the hand and led her forth into the field-path at the back of the orchard, and there he won his bride to the full content of both their hearts.

All this time the inhabitants of Crowley Castle and the quiet people of the neighbouring village of Crowley, heard but little of "The Countess," as it was their fashion to call her. Sir Mark had his letters from her, it is true, and he read them over and over again, and moaned over them, and sighed, and put them carefully away in a bundle. But they were like arrows of pain to him. None knew their contents; none, even knowing them, would have dreamed, any more than he did, for all his moans and sighs, of the utter wretchedness of the writer. Love had long since vanished from the habitation of that pair; a habitation, not a home, even in its brightest days. Love had gone out of the window, long before poverty had come in 'at the door; yet that grim visitant who never tarries in tracking a disreputable gambler had now arrived. The count lost the last remnants of his character as a man who played honourably, and thenceforth—that being pretty nearly the only sin which banished him from good society in those days—he had to play where and how he could. Theresa's money went as

her poor angry father had foretold. By-and-by, and without her consent, her jewel-box was rifled; the diamonds round the locket holding her mother's picture were wrenched and picked out by no careful hand. Victorine found Theresa crying over the poor relics;—crying at last, without disguise, as if her heart would break.

"Oh, mamma! mamma! mamma! she sobbed out, holding up the smashed and disfigured miniature as an explanation of her grief. She was sitting on the floor, on which she had thrown herself in the first discovery of the theft. Victorine sat down by her, taking her head upon her breast, and soothing her. She did not ask who had done it; she asked Theresa no question which the latter would have shrunk from answering; she knew all in that hour, without the count's name having passed the lips of either of them. And from that time she watched him as a tiger watches his prey.

When the letters came from England, the three letters from Sir Mark and the affianced bride and bridegroom, announcing the approaching marriage of Duke and Bessy, Theresa took them straight to Victorine. Theresa's lips were tightened, her pale cheeks were paler. She waited for Victorine to speak. Not a word did the Frenchwoman utter; but she smoothed the letters one over the other, and tore them in two, throwing the pieces on the ground, and stamping on them.

"Oh, Victorine!" cried Theresa, dismayed at passion that went so far beyond her own, "I never expected it—I never thought of it—but, perhaps, it was but natural."

"It was not natural; it was infamous! To have loved you once, and not to wait for chances, but to take up with that mean poor girl at the Parsonage. Pah! and her letter! Sir Mark is of my mind, though, I can see. I am sorry I tore up your letter. He feels, he knows, that Mr. Duke Brownlow ought to have waited, waited, waited. Some one waited fourteen years, did he not? The count will not live for ever."

Theresa did not see the face of wicked meaning as those last words were spoken.

Another year rolled heavily on its course of wretchedness to Theresa. That same revolution of time brought increase of peace and joy to the English couple, striving humbly, striving well, to do their duty as children to the unhappy and deserted Sir Mark. They had their reward in the birth of a little girl. Yet, close on the heels of this birth followed a great sorrow. The good parson died, after a short sudden illness. Then came the customary trouble after the death of a clergyman. The widow had to leave the Parsonage, the home of a lifetime, and seek a new resting-place for her declining years.

Fortunately for all parties, the now vicar was a bachelor; no other than the tutor who had accompanied Duke on his grand tour; and it was made a condition that he should allow the widow of his predecessor to remain at the Parsonage as his housekeeper. Bessy would fain have had her mother at the castle, and this course would have been infinitely preferred by Madam Hawtrey, who, indeed, suggested the wish to her daughter. But Sir Mark was obstinately against it; nor did he spare his caustic remarks on Madam Hawtrey, even before her own daughter. He had never quite forgiven Duke's marriage, although he was personally exceedingly fond of Bessy. He referred this marriage, in some part, and perhaps to no greater extent than was true, to madam's good management in throwing the young people together; and he was explicit in the expression of his opinion.

Poor Theresa! Every day she more and more bitterly rued her ill-starred marriage. Often and often she cried to herself, when she was alone in the dead of the night, "I cannot bear it—I cannot bear it!" But again in the daylight her pride would help her to keep her woe to herself. She could not bear the gaze of pitying eyes; she could not bear even Victorine's fierce sympathy. She might have gone home like a poor prodigal to her father, if Duke and Bessy had not, as she imagined, reigned triumphant in her place, both in her father's heart and in her father's home. And all this while, that father almost hated the tender attentions which were rendered to him by those who were not his Theresa, his only child, for whose presence he yearned and longed in silent misery. Then again (to return to Theresa), her husband had his fits of kindness towards her. If he had been very fortunate in play, if he had heard other men admire her, he would come back for a few moments to his loyalty, and would lure back the poor tortured heart, only to crush it afresh. One day—after a short time of easy temper, caresses, and levity—she found out something, I know not what, in his life, which stung her to the quick. Her sharp wits and sharper tongue spoke out most cutting insults; at first he smiled, as if rather amused to see how she was ransacking her brain to find stabbing speeches; but at length she touched some sore; he scarcely lost the mocking smile upon his face, but his eyes flashed lurid fire, and his heavy closed hand fell on her white shoulder with a terrible blow!

She stood up, facing him, fearless, deadly white. "The poor old man at home!" was all she said, trembling, shivering all over, but with her eyes fixed on his coward face. He shrank from her look, laughed aloud to hide whatever feeling might be hidden in his bosom, and left

the room. She only said again, "The poor old man—the poor old deserted, desolate man!" and felt about blindly for a chair.

She had not sat down a minute though, before she started up and rang her bell. It was Victorine's office to answer it: but Theresa looked almost surprised to see her. "You—I wanted the others—I want them all! They shall all see how their master treats his wife! Look here!" she pushed the gauze neckerchief from her shoulder—the mark was there red and swollen. Bid them all come here—Victorine, Amadée, Jean, Adèle—all will be justified by their testimony, whatever I do!" Then she fell to shaking and crying.

Victorine said nothing, but went to a certain cupboard where she kept medicines and drugs of which she alone knew the properties, and there she mixed a draught, which she made her mistress take. Whatever its nature was, it was soothing. Theresa leaned back in her chair, still sobbing heavily from time to time, until at last she dropped into a kind of doze. Then Victorine softly lifted the neckerchief, which had fallen into its place, and looked at the mark. She did not speak; but her whole face was a fearful threat. After she had looked her fill, she smiled a deadly smile. And then she touched the soft bruised flesh with her lips, much as though The resa were the child she had been twenty years ago. Soft as the touch was Theresa shivered, and started and half awoke. "Are they come?" she murmured; "Amadée, Jean, Adèle?" but without waiting for an answer she fell asleep again.

Victorine went quietly back to the cupboard where she kept her drugs, and stayed there, mixing something noiselessly. When she had done what she wanted, she returned to her mistress's bedroom, and looked at her, still sleeping. Then she began to arrange the room. No blue silk curtains and silver mirrors, now, as in the Rue Louis le Grand. A washed-out faded Indian chintz, and an old battered toilet service of Japanware; the disorderly signs of the count's late presence; an emptied flask of liqueur.

All the time Victorine arranged this room she kept saying to herself, "At last! At last!" Theresa slept through the daylight, slept late into the evening, leaning back where she had fallen in her chair. She was so motionless that Victorine appeared alarmed. Once or twice she felt her pulse, and gazed earnestly into the tear-stained face. Once, she very carefully lifted one of the eyelids, and holding a lighted taper near, peered into the eye. Apparently satisfied, she went out and ordered a basin of broth to be ready when she asked for it. Again she sat in deep silence; nothing stirred in the close chamber; but in the street the carriages began to roll, and the footmen and torch-bearers to cry aloud their masters' names and titles, to show what carriage in that narrow street below was entitled to precedence. A carriage stopped at the hotel-of which they occupied the third floor. Then the bell of their apartment rang loudly—rang violently. Victorine went out to see what it was that might disturb her darling—as she called Theresa to herself—her sleeping lady as she spoke of her to her servants.

She met those servants bringing in their master, the count, dead. Dead with a sword-wound received in some infamous struggle. Victorine stood and looked at him. "Better so," she muttered. "Better so. But, monseigneur, you shall take this with you, whithersoever your wicked soul is fleeing." And she struck him a stroke on his shoulder, just where Theresa's bruise was. It was as light a stroke as well could be; but this irreverence to the dead called forth indignation even from the hardest bearers of the body. Little recked Victorine. She turned her back on the corpse, went to her cupboard, took out the mixture she had made with so much care, poured it out upon the bare wooden floor, and smeared it about with her foot.

A fortnight later, when no news had come from Theresa for many weeks, a poor chaise was soon from the castle windows lumbering slowly up the carriage road to the gate. No one thought much of it; perhaps it was some friend of the housekeeper's; perhaps it was some humble relation of Mrs. Duke's (for many such had found out their cousin since her marriage). No one noticed the shabby carriage much, until the hall-porter was startled by the sound of the great bell pealing, and, on opening wide the hall-doors, saw standing before him the Mademoiselle Victorine of old days—thinner, sallower, in mourning. In the carriage sat Theresa, in the deep widow's weeds of those days. She looked out of the carriage-window wistfully, in beyond Joseph, the hall-porter.

"My father!" she cried, eagerly, before Victorine could speak. "Is Sir Mark—well?" ("alive" was her first thought, but she dared not give the word utterance.)

"Call Mr. Duke!" said Joseph, speaking to some one unseen. Then he came forward. "God bless you, Miss! God bless you! And this day of all days! Sir Mark is well—least-ways he's sadly changed. Where's Mr. Duke? Call him; My young lady's fainting!"

And this was Theresa's return home. None ever knew how much she had suffered since she had left home. If any one had known, Victorine would never have stood there dressed in that mourning. She put it on, sorely against her will, for the purpose of upholding the lying fiction of

Theresa's having been a prosperous marriage. She was always indignant if any one of the old servants-fell back into the once familiar appellation of Miss Theresa. "The countess," she would say, in lofty rebuke.

What passed between Theresa and her father at that first interview no one ever knew. Whether she told him anything of her married life, or whether she only soothed the tears he shed on seeing her again, by sweet repetition of tender words and caresses—such as are the sugared pabulum of age as well as of infancy—no one ever knew. Neither Duke nor his wife ever heard her allude to the time she had passed in Paris, except in the most cursory and superficial manner. Sir Mark was anxious to show her that all was forgiven, and would fain have displaced Bessy from her place as lady of the castle, and made Theresa take the headship of the house, and sit at table where the mistress ought to be. And Bessy would have given up her onerous dignities without a word; for Duke was always more jealous for his wife's position than she herself was, but Theresa declined to assume any such place in the household, saying, in the languid way which now seemed habitual to her, that English house-keeping, and all the domestic arrangements of an English country house were cumbrous and wearisome to her; that if Bessy would continue to act as she had done hitherto, and would so forestal what must be her natural duties at some future period, she, Theresa, would be infinitely obliged.

Bessy consented, and in every thing tried to remember what Theresa liked, and how affairs were ordered in the old Theresa days. She wished the servants to feel that "the countess" had equal rights with herself in the management of the house. But she, to whom the housekeeper takes her accounts—she in whose hands the power of conferring favors and privileges remains de facto —will always be held by servants as the mistress; and Theresa's claims soon sank into the background. At first, she was too broken-spirited, too languid, to care for anything but quiet rest in her father's companionship. They sat sometimes for hours hand in hand; or they sauntered out on the terraces, hardly speaking, but happy; because they were once more together, and once more on loving terms. Theresa grew strong during this time of gentle brooding peace. The pinched pale face of anxiety lined with traces of suffering, relaxed into the soft oval; the light came into the eyes, the colour came into the cheeks.

But, in the autumn after Theresa's return, Sir Mark died; it had been a gradual decline of strength, and his last moments were passed in her arms. Her new misfortune threw her back into the wan worn creature she had been when she first came home, a widow, to Crowley Castle; she shut herself up in her rooms, and allowed no one to come near her but Victorine. Neither Duke nor Bessy was admitted into the darkened rooms, which she had hung with black cloth in solemn funereal state.

Victorine's life since her return to the castle had been anything but peaceable. New powers had arisen in the housekeeper's room · Madam Brownlow had her maid, far more exacting than Madam Brownlow herself; and a new housekeeper reigned in the place of her who was formerly but an echo of Victorine's opinions. Victorine's own temper, too, was not improved by her four years abroad, and there was a general disposition among the servants to resist all her assumption of authority. She felt her powerlessness after a struggle or two, but treasured up her vengeance. If she had lost power over the household, however, there was no diminution of her influence over her mistress. It was her device at last that lured the countess out of her gloomy seclusion.

Almost the only creature Victorine cared for, besides Theresa, was the little Mary Brownlow. What there was of softness in her woman's nature seemed to come out towards children; though, if the child had been a boy instead of a girl, it is probable that Victorine might not have taken it into her good graces. As it was, the French nurse and the English child were capital friends; and when Victorine sent Mary into the countess's room, and bade her not be afraid, but ask the lady in her infantine babble to come out and see Mary's snow-man, she knew that the little one, for her sake, would put her small hand into Theresa's, and thus plead with more success, because with less purpose, than any one else had been able to plead. Out came Theresa, colourless and sad, holding Mary by the hand. They went, unobserved as they thought, to the great gallery-window, and looked out into the court-yard; then Theresa returned to her rooms. But the ice was broken, and before the winter was over, Theresa fell into her old ways, and sometimes smiled, and sometimes even laughed, until chance visitors again spoke of her rare beauty and her courtly grace.

It was noticeable that Theresa revived first out of her lassitude to an interest in all Duke's pursuits. She grew weary of Bessy's small cares and domestic talk—she, about the servants, now about her mother and the Parsonage, now about the parish. She questioned Duke about his travels, and could enter into his appreciation and judgment of foreign nations; she perceived the latent powers of his mind; she became impatient of their remaining dormant in country seclusion. She had spoken of leaving Crowley Castle, and of finding

some other home, soon after her father's death; but both Duke and Bessy had urged her to stay with them, Bessy saying, in the pure innocence of her heart, how glad she was that, in the probably increasing cares of her nursery, Duke would have a companion so much to his mind.

About a year after Sir Mark's death, the member for Sussex died, and Theresa set herself to stir up Duke to assume his place. With some difficulty (for Bessy was passive: perhaps even opposed to the scheme in her quiet way), Theresa succeeded, and Duke was elected. She was vexed at Bessy's torpor, as she called it, in the whole affair; vexed as she now often was with Bessy's sluggish interest in all things beyond her immediate ken. Once, when Theresa tried to make Bessy perceive how Duke might shine and rise in his new sphere, Bessy burst into tears, and said, "You speak as if his presence here were nothing, and his fame in London everything. I can not help fearing that he will leave off caring for all the quiet ways in which we have been so happy ever since we were married."

"But when he is here," replied Theresa, "and when he wants to talk to you of politics, of foreign news, of great public interests, you drag him down to your level of woman's cares."

"Do I?" said Bessy. "Do I drag him down? I wish I was cleverer; but you know, Theresa, I was never clever in anything but housewifery."

Theresa was touched for a moment by this humility.

"Yet, Bessy, you have a great deal of judgment, if you will but exercise it. Try and take an interest in all he cares for, as well as making him try and take an interest in home affairs."

But, somehow, this kind of conversation too often ended in dissatisfaction on both sides; and the servants gathered, from induction rather than from words, that the two ladies were not on the most cordial terms; however friendly they might wish to be, and might strive to appear. Madam Hawtrey, too, allowed her jealousy of Theresa to deepen into dislike. She was jealous because, in some unreasonable way, she had taken it into her head that Theresa's presence at the castle was the reason why she was not urged to take up her abode there on Sir Mark's death; as if there were not rooms and suits of rooms enough to lodge a wilderness of dowagers in the building, if the owner so wished. But Duke had certain ideas pretty strongly fixed in his mind; and one was a repugnance to his mother-in-law's constant company. But he greatly increased her income as soon as he had it in his power, and left it entirely to herself how she should spend it.

Having now the means of travelling about, Madam Hawtrey betook herself pretty frequently to such watering-places as were in vogue at that day, or went to pay visits at the houses of those friends who occasionally came lumbering up in shabby vehicles to visit their cousin Bessy at the castle. Theresa cared little for Madam Hawtrey's coldness; perhaps, indeed, never perceived it. She gave up striving with Bessy, too; it was hopeless to try to make her an intellectual ambitious companion to her husband. He had spoken in the House; he had written a pamphlet that made much noise; the minister of the day had sought him out and was trying to attach him to the government. Theresa, with her Parisian experience of the way in which women influenced politics, would have given anything for the Brownlows to have taken a house in London. She longed to see the great politicians, to find herself in the thick of the struggle for place and power, the brilliant centre of all what was worth hearing and seeing in the kingdom. There had been some talk of this same London house; but Bessy had pleaded against it earnestly while Theresa sat by in indignant silence, until she could bear the discussion no longer; going off to her own sitting room, where Victorine was at work. Here her pent-up words found vent—not addressed to her servant, but not restrained before her:

"I can not bear it—to see him cramped in by her narrow mind, to hear her weak selfish arguments, urged because she feels she would be out of place beside him. And Duke is hampered with this woman; he whose powers are unknown even to himself, or he would put her feeble nature on one side, and seek his higher atmosphere. How he would shine! How he does shine! Good Heaven! To think——"

And here she sank into silence, watched by Victorine's furtive eyes.

Duke had excelled all he had previously done by some great burst of eloquence, and the country rang with his words. He was to come down to Crowley Castle for a parliamentary recess, which occurred almost immediately after this. Theresa calculated the hours of each part of the complicated journey, and could have told to five minutes when he might be expected; but the baby was ill and absorbed all Bessy's attention. She was in the nursery by the cradle in which the child slep, when her husband came riding up to the castle gate. But Theresa was at the gate; her hair all out of powder, and blowing away into dishevelled curls, as the hood of her cloak fell back; her lips parted with a breathless welcome; her eyes shining out love and pride. Duke was but mortal. All London chanted his rising fame; and here in his home Theresa seemed to be the only person who appreciated him.

The servants clustered in the great hall; for it was now some length of time since he had been at home. Victorine was there, with some head-gear for her lady; and when, in reply to his inquiry for his wife, the grave butler asserted that she was with young master, who was, they feared, very seriously ill, Victorine said, with the familiarity of an old servant, and as if to assuage Duke's anxiety: "Madam fancies the child is ill, because she can think of nothing but him, and perpetual watching has made her nervous." The child, however, was really ill; and after a brief greeting to her husband, Bessy returned to her nursery, leaving Theresa to question, to hear, to sympathise. That night she gave way to another burst of disparaging remarks on poor motherly homely Bessy, and that night Victorine thought she read a deeper secret in Theresa's heart.

The child was scarcely ever out of his mother's arms; but the illness became worse, and it was nigh unto death. Some cream had been set aside for the little wailing creature, and Victorine had unwillingly used it for the making of a cosmetic for her mistress. When the servant in charge of it reproved her, a quarrel began as to their respective mistresses's right to give orders in the household. Before the dispute ended, pretty strong things had been said on both sides.

The child died. The heir was lifeless; the servants were in whispering dismay, and bustling discussion of their mourning; Duke felt the vanity of fame, as compared to a baby's life. Theresa was full of sympathy, but dared not express it to him; so tender was her heart becoming. Victorine regretted the death in her own way. Bessy lay speechless, and tearless; not caring for loving voices, nor for gentle touches; taking neither food nor drink; neither sleeping nor weeping. "Send for her mother," the doctor said; for Madam Hawtrey was away on her visits, and the letters telling her of her grandchild's illness had not reached her in the slow-delaying cross-country posts of those days. So she was sent for; by a man riding express, as a quicker and surer means than the post.

Meanwhile, the nurses, exhausted by their watching, found the care of little Mary by the day quite enough. Madam's maid sat up with Bessy for a night or two; Duke striding in from time to time through the dark hours to look at the white motionless face, which would have seemed like the face of one dead, but for the long-quivering sighs that came up from the overladen heart. The doctor tried his drugs, in vain, and then he tried again. This night, Victorine at her own earnest request, sat up instead of the maid. As usual, towards midnight, Duke came stealing in with shaded light. "Hush!" said Victorine, her finger on her lips. "She sleeps at last." Morning dawned •

faint and pale, and still she slept. The doctor came, and stole in on tip-toe, rejoicing in the effect of his drugs.' They all stood round the bed; Duke, Theresa, Victorine. Suddenly the doctor —a strange change upon him, a strange fear in his face,—felt the patient's pulse, put his ear to her open lips, called for a glass—a feather. The mirror was not dimmed, the delicate fibres stirred not. Bessy was dead.

I pass rapidly over many months. Theresa was again overwhelmed with grief, or rather, I should say, remorse; for now that Bessy was gone, and buried out of sight, all her innocent virtues, all her feminine homeliness, came vividly into Theresa's mind—not as wearisome, but as admirable, qualities of which she had been too blind to perceive the value. Bessy had been her own old companion too, in the happy days of childhood, and of innocence. Theresa rather shunned than sought Duke's company now. She remained at the castle, it is true, and Madam Hawtrey, as Theresa's only condition of continuing where she was, came to live under the same roof. Duke felt his wife's death deeply, but reasonably, as became his character. He was perplexed by Theresa's bursts of grief, knowing, as he dimly did, that she and Bessy had not lived together in perfect harmony. But he was much in London now; a rising statesman; and when, in autumn, he spent some time at the castle, he was full of admiration for the strangely patient way in which Theresa behaved towards the old lady. It seemed to Duke that in his absence Madam Hawtrey had assumed absolute power in his household, and that the high-spirited Theresa submitted to her fantasies with even more docility than her own daughter would have done. Towards Mary, Theresa was always kind and indulgent.

Another autumn came, and before it went, old ties were renewed, and Theresa's was pledged to become her cousin's wife.

There were two people strongly affected by this news when it was promulgated; one—and this was natural under the circumstances—was Madam Hawtrey; who chose to resent the marriage as a deep personal offence to herself as well as to her daughter's memory, and who sternly rejecting all Theresa's entreaties, and Duke's invitation to continue her residence at the castle, went off into lodgings in the village. The other person strongly affected by the news was Victorine.

From being a dry active energetic middle, aged woman, she now, at the time of Theresa's engagement, sank into the passive languor of advanced life. It seemed as if she felt no more need of effort, or strain, or exertion. She sought solitude; liked nothing better than to sit in her room adjoining Theresa's dressing room, sometimes sunk in a reverie, sometimes employed on an intricate piece of knitting with almost spas-

modic activity. But wherever Theresa went, thither would Victorine go. Theresa had imagined that her old nurse would prefer being left at the castle, in the soothing tranquility of the country, to accompanying her and her husband to the house in Grosvenor-square, which they had taken for the parliamentary season. But the mere offer of a choice seemed to irritate Victorine inexpressibly. She looked upon the proposal as a sign that Theresa considered her as superannuated—that her nursling was weary of her, and wished to supplant her services by those of a younger maid. It seemed impossible to dislodge this idea when it had once entered into her head, and it led to frequent bursts of temper, in which she violently upbraided Theresa for her ingratitude towards so faithful a follower.

One day, Victorine went a little further in her expressions than usual, and Theresa, usually so forbearing towards her, turned at last. "Really, Victorine!" she said, "this is misery to both of us. You say you never feel so wicked as when I am near you; that my ingratitude is such as would be disowned by fiends; what can I, what must I do? You say you are never so unhappy as when you are near me; must we, then, part? Would that be for your happiness?"

"And is that what it has come to!" exclaimed Victorine. "In my country they reckon a building secure against wind and storm and all the ravages of time, if the first mortar used has been tempered with human blood. But not even our joint secret, though it was tempered well with blood, can hold our lives together! How much less all the care, all the love, that I lavished upon you in the days of my youth and strength!"

Theresa came close to the chair in which Victorine was seated. She took hold of her hand and held it fast in her own. "Speak Victorine," said she, hoarsely, "and tell me what you mean. What is our joint secret? And what do you mean by its being a secret of blood? Speak out. I WILL know."

"As if you do not know!" replied Victorine, harshly. "You don't remember my visits to Bianconi, the Italian chemist in the Marais long ago?" She looked into Theresa's face, to see if her words had suggested any deeper meaning than met the ear. No; Theresa's look was stern, but free and innocent.

"You told me you went there to learn the composition of certain unguents, and cosmetics, and domestic medicines"

"Ay, and paid high for my knowledge, too," said Victorine, with a low chuckle. "I learned more than you have mentioned, my lady countess. I learnt the secret nature of many drugs—to speak plainly, I learnt the art of poisoning. And," suddenly standing up, "it was for your sake I learnt it. For your service—you—who would fain cast me off in my old age. For you!"

Theresa blanched to a deadly white. But she tried to move neither feature nor limb, nor to avert her eyes for one moment from the eyes that defied her. "For my service, Victorine?"

"Yes! The quieting draught was all ready for your husband when they brought him home dead!"

"Thank God his death does not lie at your door!"

"Thank God!" mocked Victorine. "The wish for his death does lie at your door; and the intent to rid you of him does lie at my door. And I am not ashamed of it. Not I! It was not for myself I would have done it, but because you suffered so. He had struck you, whom I had nursed on my breast."

"Oh, Victorine!" said Theresa, with a shudder. "Those days are past. Do not let us recall them. I was so wicked because I was so miserable; and now I am so happy, so inexpressibly happy, that—do let me try to make you happy too!"

"You ought to try," said Victorine, not yet pacified; "can't you see how the incomplete action once stopped by Fate was tried again, and with success; and how you are now reaping the benefit of my sin, if sin it was?"

"Victorine! I do not know what you mean!" But some terror must have come over her; she so trembled and so shivered.

"Do you not indeed! Madame Brownlow, the country girl from Crowley Parsonage, needed sleep, and would fain forget the little child's death that was pressing on her brain. I helped the doctor to his end. She sleeps now, and she has met her baby before this, if priests' tales are true. And you, my beauty, my queen, you reign in her stead! Don't treat the poor Victorine as if she was mad, and speaking in her madness. I have heard of tricks like that being played, when the crime was done, and the criminal of use no longer."

That evening, Duke was surprised by his wife's entreaty and petition that she might leave him, and return with Victorine and her other personal servants to the seclusion of Crowley Castle. She, the great London toast, the powerful enchantress of society, and most of all, the darling wife and true companion, with this sudden fancy for this complete retirement, and for leaving her husband when he was first fully entering into the comprehension of all that a wife might be! Was it ill health? Only last night she had been in dazzling beauty, in brilliant spirits; this morning only, she had been so merry and tender. But Theresa denied that she was in any way indisposed; and

seemed suddenly so unwilling to speak of herself, and so much depressed, that Duke saw nothing for it but to grant her wish and let her go. He missed her terribly. No more pleasant tête-à-tête breakfasts, enlivened by her sense and wit, and cheered by her pretty caressing ways. No gentle secretary now, to sit by his side through long, long hours, never weary. When he went into society, he no longer found his appearance watched and waited by the loveliest woman there. When he came home from the House at night, there was no one to take an interest in his speeches, to be indignant at all that annoyed him, and charmed and proud of all the admiration he had won. He longed for the time to come when he would be able to go down for a day or two to see his wife; for her letters appeared to him dull and flat after her bright companionship. No wonder that her letters came out of a heavy heart, knowing what she knew.

She scarcely dared to go near Victorine, whose moods were becoming as variable as though she were indeed the mad woman she had tauntingly defied Theresa to call her. At times she was miserable because Theresa looked so ill, and seemed so deeply unhappy. At other times she was jealous because she fancied Theresa shrank from her and avoided her. So, wearing her life out with passion, Victorine's health grew daily worse and worse during that summer.

Theresa's only comfort seemed to be little Mary's society. She seemed as though she could not lavish love enough upon the motherless child, who repaid Theresa's affection with all the pretty demonstrativeness of her age. She would carry the little three-year-old maiden in her arms when she went to see Victorine, or would have Mary playing about in her dressing-room, if the old Frenchwoman, for some jealous freak, would come and arrange her lady's hair with her trembling hands. To avoid giving offence to Victorine, Theresa engaged no other maid; to shun overmuch or over-frank conversation with Victorine, she always had little Mary when there was a chance of the French waiting-maid coming in. For, the presence of the child was a holy restraint even on Victorine's tongue; she would sometimes check her fierce temper, to caress the little creature playing at her knees; and would only dart a covert bitter sting at Theresa under the guise of a warning against ingratitude, to Mary.

Theresa drooped and drooped in this dreadful life. She sought out Madam Hawtrey, and prayed her to come on a long visit to the castle. She was lonely, she said, asking Madam's company as a favour to herself. Madam Hawtrey was difficult to persuade; but the more she resisted, the more Theresa entreated; and when once Madam was at the castle, her own daughter had never been so dutiful, so humble a slave to her slightest fancy as was the proud Theresa now.

Yet, for all this, the lady of the castle drooped and drooped, and when Duke came down to see his darling he was in utter dismay at her looks. Yet she said she was well enough, only tired. If she had anything more upon her mind, she refused him her confidence. He watched her narrowly, trying to forestal her smallest desires. He saw her tender affection for Mary, and thought he had never seen so lovely and tender a mother to another woman's child. He wondered at her patience with Madam Hawtrey, remembering how often his own stock had been exhausted by his mother-in-law, and how the brilliant Theresa had formerly scouted and flouted at the vicar's wife. With all this renewed sense of his darling's virtues and charms, the idea of losing her was terrible to bear.

He would listen to no pleas, to no objections. Before he returned to town, where his presence was a political necessity, he sought the best medical advice that could be had in the neighborhood. The doctors came; they could make but little out of Theresa, if her vehement assertion were true that she had nothing on her mind. Nothing.

"Humour him at least, my dear lady!" said the doctor, who had known Theresa from her infancy, but who, living at the distant county town, was only called in on the Olympian occasions of great state illnesses. "Humour your husband, and perhaps do yourself some good too, by consenting to his desire that you should have change of air. Brighthelmstone is a quiet village by the sea-side. Consent, like a gracious lady, to go there for a few weeks."

So, Theresa, worn out with opposition, consented, and Duke made all the arrangements for taking her, and little Mary, and the necessary suite of servants, to Brighton, as we call it now. He resolved in his own mind that Theresa's personal attendant should be some woman young enough to watch and wait upon her mistress, and not Victorine, to whom Theresa was in reality a servant. But of this plan, neither Theresa nor Victorine knew anything until the former was in the carriage with her husband some miles distant from the castle. Then he, a little exultant in the good management by which he supposed he had spared his wife the pain and trouble of decision, told her that Victorine was left behind, and that a new accomplished London maid would await her at her journey's end.

Theresa only exclaimed, "O! What will Victorine say?" and covered her face, and sat shivering and speechless.

What Victorine did say, when she found out

the trick, as she esteemed it, that had been played upon her, was too terrible to repeat. She lashed herself up into an ungoverned passion; and then became so really and seriously ill that the servants went to fetch Madam Hawtrey in terror and dismay. But when that lady came, Victorine shut her eyes, and refused to look at her. "She has got her daughter in her hand! I will not look!" Shaking all the time, she uttered these awe-stricken words, as if she were in an ague-fit. "Bring the countess back to me. Let her face the dead woman standing there. I will not do it. They wanted her to sleep—and so did the countess, that she might step into her lawful place. Theresa, Theresa, where are you? You tempted me. What I did, I did in your service. And you have gone away, and left me alone with the dead woman! It was the same drug as the doctor gave, after all—only he gave little, and I gave much. My lady the countess spent her money well when she sent me to the old Italian to learn his trade. Lotions for the complexion, and a discriminating use of poisonous drugs. I discriminated, and Theresa profited; and now she is his wife, and has left me here alone with the dead woman. Theresa, Theresa, come back and save me from the dead woman!"

Madam Hawtrey stood by, horror-stricken.— "Fetch the vicar," said she, under her breath, to a servant.

"The village doctor is coming," said some one near. "How she raves! Is it delirium?"

"It is no delirium," said Bessy's mother. "Would to Heaven it were!"

Theresa had a happy day with her husband at Brighthelmstone before he set off on his return to London. She watched him riding away, his servant following with his portmanteau. Often and often did Duke look back at the figure of his wife, waving her handkerchief, till a turn of the road hid her from his sight. He had to pass through a little village not ten miles from his home, and there a servant, with his letters and further luggage, was to await him. There he found a mysterious, imperative note, requiring his immediate presence at Crowley Castle. Something in the awe-stricken face of the servant from the castle, led Duke to question him. But all he could say was, that Victorine lay dying, and that Madam Hawtrey had said that after that letter the master was sure to return, and so would need no luggage. Something lurked behind, evidently. Duke rode home at speed. The vicar was looking out for him. "My dear boy," said he, relapsing into the old relations of tutor and pupil, "prepare yourself."

"What for?" said Duke, abruptly; for the

being told to prepare himself, without being told for what, irritated him in his present mood. "Victorine is dead?"

"No! She says she will not die until she has seen you, and got you to forgive her, if Madam Hawtrey will not. But first read this: it is a terrible confession, made by her before me, a magistrate, believing herself to be on the point of death!"

Duke read the paper—containing little more in point of detail than I have already given—the horrible words taken down, in the short-hand in which the vicar used to write his mild prosy sermons: his pupil knew the character of old.— Duke read it twice. Then he said: "She is raving, poor creature!" But for all that, his heart's blood ran cold, and he would fain not have faced the woman, but would rather have remained in doubt to his dying day.

He went up the steps three stairs at a time, and then turned and faced the vicar, with a look like the stern calmness of death. "I wish to see her alone." He turned out all the watching women, and then he went to the bedside where Victorine sat, half propped up with pillows, watching all his doings and his looks, with her hollow awful eyes. "Now, Victorine, I will read this paper aloud to you. Perhaps your mind has been wandering; but you understand me now?" A feeble murmur of assent met his listening ear. "If any statement in this paper be not true, make me a sign. Hold up your hand—for God's sake hold up your hand. And if you can, do it with truth in this, your hour of dying, Lord have mercy upon you; but if you cannot hold up your hand, then Lord have mercy upon me!"

He read the paper slowly; clause by clause he read the paper. No sign; no uplifted hand. At the end he spoke, and he bent his head to listen. "The Countess—Theresa you know—she who has left me to die alone—she"—then mortal strength failed, and Duke was left alone in the chamber of death.

He stayed in the chamber many minutes, quite still. Then he left the room, and said to the first domestic he could find, "The woman is dead. See that she is attended to." But he went to the vicar and had a long talk with him. He sent a confidential servant for little Mary—on some pretext, hardly careful, or plausible enough; but his mood was desperate, and he seemed to forget almost everything but Bessy, his first wife, his innocent, girlish bride.

Theresa could ill spare her little darling, and was perplexed by the summons; but an explanation of it was to come in a day or two. It came.

"Victorine is dead! I need say no more. She could not carry her awful secret into the next world, but told all. I can think of nothing but my poor Bessy, delivered over to the cruelty of such a woman. And you, Theresa, I leave you to your conscience, for you have slept in my bosom. Henceforward I am a stranger to you. By the time you receive this, I, and my child, and that poor murdered girl's mother, will have left England. What will be our next step I know not. My agent will do for you what you need."

Theresa sprang up and rang the bell with mad haste. "Get me a horse!" she cried, "and bid William be ready to ride with me for his life—for my life—along the coast, to Dover!"

They rode and they galloped through the night, scarcely staying to bait their horse. But when they came to Dover, they looked out to sea upon the white sails that bore Duke and his child away. Theresa was too late, and it broke her heart. She lies buried in Dover church-yard. After long years Duke returned to England; but his place in parliament knew him no more, and his daughter's husband sold Crowley Castle to a stranger.

III.

HOW THE SIDE-ROOM WAS ATTENDED BY A DOCTOR.

How the Doctor found his way into our society, none of us can tell. It did not occur to us to inquire into the matter at the time, and now the point is lost in the dim obscurity of the past. We only know that he appeared suddenly and mysteriously. It was shortly after we had formed our Mutual Admiration Society, in this very room in Mrs. Lirriper's Lodgings. We were discussing things in general in our usual amiable way, admiring poets, worshipping heroes, and taking all men and all things for what they seemed. We were young and ingenuous, pleased with our own ideas, and with each other's; full of belief and trust in all things good and noble, and with no hatred, save for what was false, and base, and mean. In this spirit we were commenting with indignation upon a new heresy with regard to the age of the world, when a strange voice broke in upon our conversation:

"I beg your pardon; you are wrong. The age of the world is exactly three millions eight hundred and ninety-seven thousand four hundred and twenty-five years, eight months, fourteen days, nine hours, thirty-five minutes, and seventeen seconds."

At the first sound of this mysterious voice we all looked up, and perceived standing on the hearth-rug before the fire by which you sit, Major, a little closely knit, middle-aged man, dressed in black. He had a hooked nose, piercing black eyes, and a grizzled beard, and his head was covered with a shock of crisp dark hair. Our first impulse was to resent the stranger's interference as an impertinence, and to demand what business he had in that room in Mrs. Lirriper's house, sacred to the social meetings of the Mutual Admiration Society? But we no sooner set eyes upon him than the impulse was checked, and we remained for a minute or so gazing upon the stranger in silence. We saw at a glance that he was no mere meddling fool. He was considerably older than any of us there present, his face beamed with intelligence, his eyes sparkled with humor, and his whole expression was that of a man confident of mental strength and superiority. The look on his face seemed to imply that he had reckoned us all up in an instant. So much were we impressed by the stranger's appearance, that we quite forgot the queries which had naturally occurred to us when he interrupted our conversation: Who are you? Where do you belong to? How did you come here? It was allowable for a member of the society to introduce a friend; but none of us had introduced him, and we were the only members in the room.— None of us had seen him enter, nor had we been conscious of his presence until we heard his voice. On comparing notes afterwards, it was found that the same thought had flitted across all our minds. Had he come down the chimney? Or up through the floor? But at the time, as we saw no smoke and smelt no brimstone, we dismissed the suspicion for the more natural explanation that some member had introduced him, and had gone away, leaving him there. I was mentally framing a civil question with the view of elucidating this point, when the stranger, who spoke with a foreign accent, again addressed us:

"I trust," said he, "I am not intruding upon your society: but the subject of your discussion is one that I have studied deeply, and I was betrayed into a remark by—by my enthusiasm: I beg you will pardon me."

He said this so affably, and with so much dignified politeness of an elderly kind, that we were all disarmed, and protested, in a body, that there was no occasion for any apology. And it followed upon this, in some sort of insensible way, that the stranger came and took a seat among us, and spent the evening with us, proving a match for us in the airy gaiety of our discussions, and more than a match for us in all kinds of knowledge. We were all charmed with the stranger, and he appeared to be highly pleased with us. When he went away he shook hands with us with marked cordiality and warmth, and left us his card. It bore this inscription:

Doctor Goliath, Ph.D.

After this, the doctor regularly frequented our society, and we took his coming as a matter of course; being quite content to accept his great learning and numerous accomplishments as a certificate of his eligibility for membership in our fraternity. It was no wonder that we came to look upon the doctor as a great personage. His fund of knowledge was inexhaustible. He seemed to know everything—not generally and in a superficial manner—but particularly and minutely. It was not, however, by making a parade of his knowledge that he gave us this impression. He let it out incidentally, as occasion required. If language were the topic, the doctor, by a few offhand remarks, made it plain to us that he was acquainted with almost every language under the sun. He spoke English with an accent which partook of the character of almost every modern tongue. If law came up, he could discourse of codes and judgments with the utmost familiarity, citing act, chapter, and section, as if the whole study of his life had been law. So with politics, history, geology, chemistry, mechanics, and even medicine. Nothing came amiss to Doctor Goliah. He was an animated Cyclopædia of universal knowledge. But there was nothing of the pedant about him. He treated his learning as bagatelle; he threw off his knowledge as other people throw off jokes: he was only serious when he mixed a salad, brewed a bowl of punch, or played a game of piquet. He was not at all proud of being able to translate the Ratcatcher's Daughter into six languages, including Greek and Arabic; but he believed he was the only man on the face of the earth who knew the exact proportions of oil and vinegar requisite for the proper mixture of a potato-salad. He was learned in the highest degree; yet he had all the reckless jollity of a schoolboy, and could talk nonsense and make sport of wisdom and philosophy better than any of us. He took our society by storm; he became an oracle; we quoted him as an authority, and spoke of him as the doctor, as if there were no other doctor on the face of the earth.

Shortly before the doctor's appearance among us, we, the members of the Mutual Admiration Society, had sworn eternal friendship. We had vowed ever to love each other, ever to believe in each other, ever to be true and just and kindly towards each other, and never to be estranged one from another, either by prosperity or adversity. As a sign and symbol of our brotherhood, we had agreed to call each other by familiar and affectionate abbreviations of our christian names; and, in pursuance of this amiable scheme, we had arranged to present each other with loving-cups. As we were a society of little wealth, except in the matter of loving-kindness and mutual admiration, it was resolved that the cups should be fashioned of pewter, of the measure of one quart, and each with two handles. The order was given, the loving-cups were made, and each bore an inscription in this wise: "To Tom from Sam, Jack, Will, Ned, Charley, and Harry, a token of Friendship;" the inscription being only varied as regarded the relative positions of donors and recipient. The cups were all ready, and nothing remained to be done but to pay the money and bring them away from the shop of our Benvenuto Cellini, which was situated in the parish of St. Martin's-in-the-Fields. A delay, however, occurred, owing to circumstances which I need not particularise further than to say, that they were circumstances over which we had no control.

The delay, owing to the obduracy of these uncontrollable circumstances, continued for some weeks, when, one evening, Tom came in with a large brown paper parcel under his arm. It was a parcel of strange and unwonted aspect.

"Ha! ha!" cried the doctor, "what have we here? Say, my Tom, is it something to eat, something to drink, something perchance to smoke? For in such things only doth my soul delight."

"I don't believe you when you say that, doctor," said Tom, quite seriously; for Tom had fallen more prostrate than any of us before the doctor's great character.

"Not believe me?" cried the doctor. "I mean it. Man, sir, is an animal whose only misfortune is, that he is endowed with the accursed power of thinking. If I were not possessed by his evil spirit of Thought, do you know what I would do?"

Tom could form no idea what he would do.

"Well, then," said the doctor, "I would lie all day in the sun, and eat potatoe-salad out of a trough!"

"What! like a pig?" Tom exclaimed.

"Yes, like a pig," said the doctor. "I never see a pig lying on clean straw, with his snout poked into a delightful mess of barley-meal and cabbage-leaves, but I become frightfully envious!"

"Oh, doctor!" we all exclaimed in chorus.

"Fact. I say to myself, How much better off, how much happier is this pig than I! To obtain my potatoe-salad, without which life would be a blank, I have to do a deed my soul abhors. I have to work. The pig has no work to do for that troughful of barley-meal and cabbage-leaves. Because I am an animal endowed with power of thought and reason, I was sent to school and taught to read. See what misfortune, what misery, that has brought upon me! You laugh, but I am driven to read books, and parliamentary debates, and leading articles. I was induced the

other day to attend a social congress. If I had been a pig, I should not have had to endure that."

"Ah, but, doctor," said Tom, "the pig has no better part."

The doctor burst into a yell of exultation!

"What! The pig no better part? Ha! ha! Sir, the better part of a pig is pork. The butcher comes to me, and to the pig alike: but what remains of me when he has done his foll work? You put me in a box and screw me down, and stow me away out of sight; and you pretend to grieve for me. But the pig—you eat him, and rejoice in earnest! And that reminds me that I shall have a pork-chop for supper. By the way, is it a lettuce you have in that paper parcel, Tom?"

"It is not a lettuce, doctor."

"Not a lettuce! Ha! I see something glitter —precious metal—gold? no, silver! to obtain which, in a commensurate quantity, I would commit crimes—murder!"

"Oh, doctor," said Tom, "you are giving yourself a character which you don't deserve."

"Am I?" said the doctor. You don't know me. And after all, what is murder? Nothing. You kill two or three of your fellow-creatures—a dozen, for that matter; what then? There are plenty more. Do you know what is the population of the earth? I will tell you. Exactly one thousand three hundred millions eight hundred and ninety-nine thousand six hundred and twenty souls. How many murders are committed in the course of a year do you imagine? You think only those you read of in the newspapers. Bah! An intimate knowledge of the subject enables me to inform you that the number of murders committed in Great Britain and Ireland, and the Channel Islands, annually amounts to fifteen thousand seven hundred and forty-five. It is one of the laws of nature for keeping down the population. Every man who commits a murder obeys this law."

Tom's hair was beginning to stand on end, for the doctor said all this with a terrible fierceness of manner. His strange philosophy was not without its effect upon the rest of us. We had been accustomed to a good deal of freedom in our discussions, but we had never ventured upon anything so audacious as this.

"Come, Tom," said the doctor, "unveil your treasure, and let me see if it be worth my while lying in wait for you in the dark lanes as you go home to-night."

"Well, no, it isn't doctor," said Tom, "for the article is only of pewter." And Tom uncovered his loving-cup. Circumstances had relented in Tom's case, and he had gone and paid for his own loving-cup.

"Pewter!" said the doctor. "Bah! it is not worth my while; but if it had been silver, now, why then I might——" And the doctor put on a diabolical expression, that seemed to signify highway robbery accompanied with violence, and murder followed by immediate dissection. Presently the doctor noticed the inscription "Ha! ha!" he said, "what is this?" An inscription! 'To Tom, from Sam, Jack, Will, Ned, Charley, and Harry—a token of Friendship.' Friendship! Ha! ha! 'tis but a name, an empty name, a mockery, a delusion, and a snare. I tell you there is no such thing in the world."

"Oh, don't say that, doctor!" cried Tom, looking quite hurt.

"Ah, returned the doctor, "you will find it out. I have always found it out ; and since I formed my first friendship and was deceived—it is now—let me see how many years ?—one thousand eight hundred and—but no matter."

The doctor paused, as if oppressed with painful recollections.

"Ned," said Sam, leaning across to me, "do you know what I think the doctor is ?"

"No," I said.

"Well," he said, "hang'd if I don't think he is the Wandering Jew. Look at his boots !"

I looked at his boots. They were not neat boots : that was all I perceived about them.

"Don't you observe," said Sam, "how flat and trodden down they are? The' doctor has done a deal of walking in those boots. Mark their strange and ancient shape! Look at the dust upon them —it is the dust of centuries !"

The doctor was roaring with laughter at the idea of our mutual presentation scheme, and was calling us "innocents," and Tom's loving cup a "mug."

Tom was getting red in the face and looking ashamed. In fact, we were all looking rather sheepish: for it had never struck us until now, how silly and sentimental we all were. We said nothing to the doctor about the six other loving-cups that were waiting to be paid for and claimed ; and when Tom, with a face as red as a coal, covered up his "mug" as the doctor called it and put it away, we were glad to change the subject, to escape from our embarrassment. We were so thoroughly ashamed of ourselves, that we endeavoured to redeem our characters in the eyes of the doctor, by plunging recklessly into any depth of cynical opinion that he choose to sound. And the doctor, in the course of time, led us to the very bottom of the pit of cynicism. As we listened to him, and held converse with him day after day, we began to see how very green and unsophisticated we had all been. We came to know that the poets and heroes whom we had worshipped were nothing but humbugs and pretenders ; that the great statesmen whom we had believed in and

admired, were blunderers or traitors ; that the mighty potentates whose power and sagacity we had extolled, were tyrannical miscreants, or puppets in the hands of others ; that the philanthropists whom all men praised, were conceited self-seeking hypocrites : that the patriots whose names we had reverenced in common with all the world, were scoundrels of the deepest dye. The doctor's influence led us on insensibly, step by step. How could we resist it ? It was a fascination. He knew everything, could prove everything, and had such a store of facts that we had never heard of in support of his conclusions, that it was impossible, with our limited knowledge, to withstand him. We were shocked at first ; but, as the revolution proceeded, we got used to the sight of blood, and saw the heads of our heroes fall with the utmost indifference. At length we came to revel in it, and sought for new victims, that we might demolish them, and do our despite upon them. The doctor led the way more boldly as we advanced. He hinted darkly at crimes in which he had had a hand, and at crimes which he would yet commit when the opportunity arrived. Whenever a murder was committed, the doctor was the friend and advocate of the murderer, and vowed fierce vengeance against the judge and jury who condemned him to be hanged. When news of war and disaster came, he rubbed his hands and gloated over it with glee, because he had prophesied what would happen through the imbecility and treason of infamous scoundrels who called themselves statesmen and generals.

From a Mutual Admiration Society we became a society of iconoclasts. Tom and Jack, and Sam and Harry, and the rest of us, who had begun by swearing eternal friendship, were now bitter disputants, despising each other's mental qualities, calling each other duffers behind each other's backs, and laughing all the old modest pretensions to scorn. The loving-cups had faded out of memory. I passed the shop of our Benvenuto Cellini, the pewterer, one day, and saw the whole six exposed in the window for sale. I called upon Tom, to show him an article demolishing a popular author whom we had once idolized, and I noticed his loving-cup stowed away under the table with a waste-paper-basket and a spittoon. It had grown dull and battered, like a public-house pot, and was filled with short black pipes, and matches, and ends of cigars, and rubbish. I kicked it playfully with my foot, and laughed ; and Tom blushed and put it away out of sight.

Our society, in its new form, prospered exceedingly. We became famous for the freedom of our speech and the audacity of our opinions. We spent all our leisure hours together, and our defiant discussion kept us in a constant state of mental intoxication. But a sober moment arrived.

Tom and I sat together, one gloomy day, alone. We were solemn and moody, and smoked in silence. At length Tom said:

"Ned, I passed the shop to-day, and saw those six loving-cups in the window."

I replied, fretfully, "Bother the loving-cups!"

"No," said Tom "I have other thoughts at this present moment; I have had them often, but have smothered them—smothered them ruthlessly, Ned; but they have always come to life again. They are very lively to-night—owing, perhaps, to the fog, or the state of my liver, or the state of my conscience—and I can't smother them."

"What do you mean, Tom?"

"You remember when we ordered the cups?"

"Yes."

'The doctor came among us shortly afterwards?'

"He did."

"And we didn't carry out our intention."

"No. You paid for yours, Tom, and brought it away, but the rest are still unredeemed pledges of affection."

"Exactly," said Tom; "and that was owing to the doctor. He laughed at us. He made us ashamed of ourselves. He made me ashamed of myself. But I had paid for my cup, and brought it away, and the thing was done. If I had not done it when I did, I should never have done it. What were we ashamed of?"

"Silliness," I said.

"No, kindness and good feeling, which we can't have too much of it in this short journey."

I did not answer. Tom went on.

"This doctor has upset us all. He has changed our nature. He has turned the milk of human kindness that was in us, sour. He is a very fascinating person, I grant; but who is he? None of us know. He came among us mysteriously; we accepted him without question. Yet we don't know any thing about him. We don't know what he is; what he does; where he lives; or even what country he belongs to."

"Well?"

"Well, I sometimes think he is the devil. He is very pleasant, but he is diabolical in all his views and opinions, nevertheless. If he is not the devil, he has, at any rate, played the devil with us. I feel it at quiet moments like these, when we are not excited and bandying flippant jokes and unbelieving sarcasms."

I smoked for a few moments in silence, and I then said:

"I feel it, too, exactly as you do, Tom. I have wished to say so often, only—only I didn't like."

"Ned that is exactly what I have felt. Suppose we take courage now."

"Suppose we do," I said.

"Very well, then," said Tom. "Let us find out who this Doctor Goliath is, what he is, and all about him."

Tom had scarcely said the words when the doctor came in. He had a small bag in his hand, and a parcel under his arm.

"I am not going to stay this evening," he said. "I have work to do—work that the world will hear of. Ha?" And he contracted his brows darkly, and laid his finger on his nose in a portentous manner.

"Good night," he said; "if I survive, well and good; if not, remember me—but as to that, I don't imagine for a moment that you will do any thing of the sort. You will say 'poor wretch,' and then go on with your jokes and sport. 'Tis the way of this vile world, which has been a huge mistake from the beginning. Farewell."

"Ned," said Tom, "let us follow him."

We did so. We followed him into the Strand and on to the bridge, where he had an altercation with the toll-keeper. We could hear the words "swindle," "imposition," "highway robbery;" and we saw the doctor's face under the lamp glaring savagely at the man. At length he flung down his halfpenny, and walked hurriedly on, but stopped abruptly at the first recess, turned into it, and looked over the parapet at the river. We had long seriously entertained the suspicion—among many others of a like kind—that the doctor knew something about the mysterious, and as yet undiscovered, murder, which is associated with that spot. He had hinted at it often.

"Look!" said Tom. "Fascination draws him to the scene of his crime.—I almost wish he would throw himself over."

But the doctor did no such thing. After looking down at the river for a few moments, he leaped off the stone ledge, and passed on. We followed at a safe distance, and kept him in sight through a great many narrow and gloomy streets, where our only guide was the dark figure moving like a shadow before us. At length the doctor turned up a narrow passage, and disappeared. We ran forward to the entrance, but the passage was completely dark, and we could see nothing. We hesitated for a moment, but immediately summoned up courage and followed, groping our way in the dark with the assistance of the wall. On coming out at the other end of this dark tunnel, we found ourselves in a triangular court lighted by a single gas-lamp placed at the apex of the triangle. There seemed to be no entrace to it save the narrow passage through which we had passed. All these strange and mysterious characteristics of the place we were enabled to see at a glance, by the aid of the one gas-lamp that stood like a mark of admiration in the corner. And that glance took in the cloudy figure of the doctor standing at a door in the darkest nook of the court, knocking. He was admitted before we reached the spot, but we had marked the house. It was number thirteen.

"An ogglesome number," said Tom. And there was an ogglesome plaster head over the doorway— a head, with a leer upon its face, and a reckoning-up expression, just like the doctor's. It seemed to be laughing at the fool's errand we had come upon.

I said, "What are we to do now?"

"Well, really, I don't know," said Tom.

"Stop," I cried; "I see a bill in the window. What does it say?"

Tom suggested, "Mangling done," as being most appropriate to a house inhabited by Doctor Goliath.

But it was not mangling. It was "Lodgings to Let for a Single Gentleman."

"Let us knock," I said, "and inquire about the lodgings, and ascertain what sort of a place it is."

We saw a light pass in the first floor. That was evidently the doctor's room, and he had gone up-stairs. We waited a little, and then knocked. The door was opened by an elderly lady of exceedingly benignant aspect, who wore the remnant of a smile upon her face. The smile was evidently not intended for us, but we took it as if it were, and reciprocated with a smiling inquiry about the lodgings. Would we step in and look at them? They were two rooms down stairs : a sitting-room and a bed-room. As the elderly lady, with a candle in her hand, was leading the way along the passage, the doctor called from above.

"Mrs. Mavor, I want you here directly."

"Excuse me a moment, gentlemen," said Mrs. Mavor; "the doctor, my first-floor lodger, has just come in, and wants his coffee. Pray take a seat in the parlour."

Mrs. Mavor left us, and went up-stairs, and the next moment we heard the doctor saying in loud and angry tones :

"Where is my spider? How dare you sweep away my spider with your murderous broom?"

"Oh, the nasty thing!" we hear Mrs. Mavor begin to say, but the doctor would not let her speak.

"Nasty thing! That's your opinion. What do you suppose that spider's opinion is of you, when you come and bring his house about his ears in the midst of his industry? How would you like it? Let me tell you that spider had as much right to live as you have; more—more! He was industrious which you are not; he had a large family to support, which you have not; and if he did spread a net to catch the flies, don't you hang up 'Lodgings to Let,' and take in single young men, like myself, and do for them? You are a heartless, wicked woman,

Mrs. Mavor."

Mrs. Mavor came down almost immediately, laughing.

"That's my first-floor lodger, Doctor Goliath," she said; "he has strange ways in some things, and pretends to get in an awful temper if any one touches his pets; but he is such a good kind soul!"

Tom and I began to stare.

"He has been with me now over seven years," Mrs. Mavor continued, "and he has behaved so well to me, and as been so kind to me when I have been ill, that nothing should induce me to take any person into the house that might disturb him or put him out of his ways. If the doctor were to leave Povis-place, I am sure I don't know what all the neighbours and the poor people about here would do; for he doctors them when they are ill, and he advises them when they are well, and he writes letters for them, and gets up subscriptions for them when there's any misfortune; and the children they're wild after him! Very often you'll see him here in the place, when he has been the gentlest and best of friends to their fathers and mothers, playing games with them, and a score of romping boys and girls on the top of his back—but he don't mind; he's so good natured, and so fond of children!"

Tom and I were opening our eyes wider and wider. The doctor called again : "Mrs. Mavor, bring me a ball of worsted, and let it be nice and soft."

Mrs. Mavor went up stairs with the worsted, and came back smiling.

"He has got his dumb pets around him now," she said, "and one of them has had an accident, and he can't bear to see the poor creature suffer. He is so tender-hearted!"

Tom and I were speechless. The doctor's pets, what could they be? Imps?

I said to Mrs. Mavor, that we had heard of Doctor Goliath, that he was a very learned and skilful man, and that we would like to have a peep at him, if she would permit us. Mrs. Mavor hesitated. He would be angry, she said, if he knew it. We put it upon our admiration for the man, and she consented; but we were only to peep through the door, and were not to make a noise.

We went up stairs quietly to the doctor's landing. His door was ajar, and we could see nearly half the room through the crack, without being seen. If it had been possible to open our eyes any wider, we should have done it now.

For, the doctor was seated at a table on which his tea-things were laid. A canary bird sat perched upon his head, a kitten was sporting at his feet, and he himself was occupied in binding up the leg of a guinea-pig.

"Poor little thing!" he was saying. "I am so sorry, so sorry; but never mind. There, there! I will bind up its poor little leg, and it will get well and run about as nicely as ever.— Ah, little cat; now you know what I told you about that canary-bird. If you kill that canary-bird, I shall kill you. That is the law of Moses, little cat: it is a cruel law, I think, but I am afraid I should have to put it in force; for I love that little bird, and I love you, too, little cat, so you will not kill my pretty canary, will you? Sweet, sweet!" And the bird, perched upon the doctor's head, was answering "Sweet, sweet!"

Mrs. Mavor was behind us, calling to us in a loud whisper to come away. We astonished Mrs. Mavor and her lodger both. We walked right into the doctor's room.

He started at the sound of our footsteps; and when he saw us he turned pale with anger.

"What means this—this unwarrantable—this impertinent intrusion?"

He poured such a volley of angry words upon us that we were confused, and scarcely knew how to act. I saw that the only course was to take the bull by the horns.

"Doctor," I said, "you are an old humbug."

"What do you mean; what do you mean, sir? How dare you!" returned the doctor.

"And I say so too," struck in the mild Tom, who had never before been known to speak so bold; doctor, you are an old humbug."

"Well, upon my word," said the doctor, "the audacity of the proceeding——"

"Who taught us to be audacious, doctor?" Tom asked, before he could finish a sentence.

The doctor gave way. He laughed, and he looked sheepish—as sheepish as we had looked when he discovered our loving-cup scheme. He scarcely knew what to say, and he put on a fierce look again, and called Mrs. Mavor.

"How dare you allow strangers to enter my room in this manner? Take that bird and that mischievous cat and that nasty guinea pig away, directly."

"It's of no use, doctor," said Tom; "we have found you out, and you can't deceive us any more. I have thought until now that you were an incarnate fiend, but I find that you belong to the other side." Tom evidently meant that the doctor was a sort of angel, but he did not use the word; being probably struck with the incongruity of associating an angelic embodiment with a wide-awake hat and Blucher boots.

The doctor laughed: which encouraged Tom to address a moral lesson, on the doctor's conduct, to Mrs. Mavor.

"To all of us, Mrs. Mavor, he has made himself out a diabolical person: fierce, bloodthirsty,

cruel. We had made a little Paradise among ourselves, and he entered it, like the beguiling serpent, and made us all wicked and unhappy. What did he do it for?"

Mrs. Mavor, seeing that the doctor was getting the worst of it, plucked up courage and spoke out. "He does it everywhere beyond the boundaries of Povis-place, and I'll tell you what he does it for. *He is ashamed of being good, and kind, and tender-hearted!*"

"A pretty thing to be ashamed of," said Tom. "I've half a mind to punch his head!"

"No, don't," said the doctor, laughing. "Sit down and have a cup of coffee, and then Mrs. Mavor will come and join us in a game of whist, and we'll have a potato-salad for supper, and I'll brew such a bowl of punch as I flatter myself no man on the face of the earth besides myself——"

"Doctor," said Tom again, "you're a humbug."

We told all to the society, and the next time the doctor came among us at Mrs. Lirriper's here, he was received with shouts of derisive welcome.

The doctor gave a party in Povis-place, and we were all invited. There was so much victuals, there were so many bottles of German wine, and there was so large a number of guests, that Mrs. Mavor's small tenement was in some danger of bursting. If I remember rightly, the provisions were on the scale of a ham and two fowls and a dozen of hocheimer, to each guest: to say nothing of the potato-salad, which was made in a bran new wash-hand basin, purchased for the occasion.

And after supper there was a presentation. The loving-cups has been redeemed; and one more was added to the number; and there they were, all bright and glittering—having been rubbed expressly for the occasion—in a row upon the table. And the extra one was inscribed, "To the Doctor, from Tom, Ned, Sam, Will, Jack, Charley and Harry, a Token of Friendship and Esteem."

Though our old heroes and idols are all set up on their pedestals long ago, Major, we are still given to cynical and audacious talk in our society, which is still held in my room here. But it deceives no one; and when the doctor tries to be fierce, he blushes at the feeble and foolish attempt he is making to conceal the tenderness of the kindest heart that ever beat.

IV.

HOW THE SECOND FLOOR KEPT A DOG.

MRS. LIRRIPER rather objects to dogs, you say, Major? Very natural in a London house.

Shall I tell you why I hope she will not object to my dog, Major? Help yourself. So I will.

"Ah, but, to goodness, look you, will her bite?" exclaimed an old Welshwoman, as she pulled her big hat further on her head, and looked askance at the big black dog which the man sitting next her had just hauled on to the coach-roof.

"It isn't a her, and he won't bite," was the sententious reply of the dog's master.

Not a pleasant-looking man, this; tall and thin, whiskerless and sallow faced; his head looking more like a bladder of lard surmounted by a scratch-wig, than anything human: dressed all in black, with a stiff shiny hat, beaver gloves, and thick lustreless Wellington boots. He had enormous collars encircling his face and growing peakedly out of a huge black silk cravat; he had a black satin waistcoat and a silver watch-guard, and an umbrella in a shiny oilskin case, and a hard slippery cold black cowskin bag, with J. M. upon it in staring white letters; and he looked very much like what he was—Mr. John Mortiboy, junior partner in the house of Crump and Mortiboy, Manchester warehouse-man, Friday-street, Cheapside, London.

What brought Mr. John Mortiboy into Wales to spend his holidays, or what induced such a pillar of British commerce to encumber himself with a dog, is no business of ours, Major. All I know, is, that he had been set down at the Barberth-road station, had dragged the black cowskin bag from under his seat, had released the dog from a square bare receptacle which the animal had filled with howls, and had mounted himself and his dog on to the top of the coach travelling towards the little watering-place of Penethly. The dog, a big black retriever, lay on the coach-roof with his fine head erect, now gazing round the landscape, now dropping his cold muzzle between his paws and taking snatches of sleep. His master sat on the extreme edge of the seat, with one Wellington boot very much displayed and dangling in the air, and he, the Welling-ton boot's owner, apparently deriving much en-joyment from the suction of his umbrella-handle. He cast his big eyes round him now and then at certain portions of the scenery pointed out by the coachman, and expressed his opinion that it was "handsome," but beyond that never vouch-safed a word until the coach drew up at the Royal Inn at Penethly, when he went at once round to the stables and superintended the preparation of a meal for his dog, then ordered a "point steak well beat, potatoes, and a pint of sherry," to be ready for him in an hour's time; inquired the way to Albion Villa; and set off for Albion Villa accompanied by his dog Beppo.

I don't think Mr. John Mortiboy was much wanted at Albion Villa, nor that he was exactly the kind of man who would have suited its in-mates. They were little conscious of the ap-proach of his hard creaking boots, striding over the ill-paved High-street of the little town, and were enjoying themselves after their own simple fashion. The blinds were down, the candles were lighted, and Mrs. Barford was pretending to be knitting, but really enjoying a placid sleep; Ellen, her eldest daughter, was reading a mag-azine; Kate, her youngest, was making some sketches under the observant tuition of a slim gentleman with a light beard, who apparently took the greatest interest in his pupil. Upon this little group the clang of the gate bell, the creaking of Mr. John Mortiboy's boots, and the strident tones of Mr. John Mortiboy's voice, fell uncomfortable. "Say Mr. John Mortiboy, of London," he exclaimed, while yet in the little pas-sage outside. The startled Welsh servant having obeyed him, he followed close upon her heels into the room.

"Servant, ladies!" said he, with a short circu-lar nod, "servant, Mrs. Barford? Best to explain matters wholesale. You wonder who I am. You're sister-in-law to my uncle, Jonas Crump. I'm my uncle's partner in Friday-street. Done too much; rather baked in the head—heavy con-signments and sitting up late at night poring over figures. The doctor recommended change of air; uncle Crump recommended Penethly, and mentioned you. I came down here, and have taken the liberty of calling. Down, Beppo! Don't mind him, miss, he wont hurt you."

"Oh! I'm not afraid of the dog!" said Ellen, with a slight start at Mr. Mortiboy's general manner, and at his calling her "Miss." Kate looked on in wonder, and the slim gentleman with the light beard confided to the said beard the word "Brute."

We're—very—pleased to see you, Mr. Mor-tiboy," said Mrs. Barford, "and—and hope that you will soon recover your health in our quiet village. I'm sure anything that we can—can do —my daughters, Miss Ellen, Miss Kate Barford; a friend of ours, Mr. Sandham—we shall be most happy to——" As Mrs. Barford's voice died away in the contemplation of the happiness before her, the young ladies and Mr. Sandham bowed, and Mr. Mortiboy favoured them with a series of short nods. Then he said, abruptly turning to the slim gentleman, "In the army, sir?"

"No, sir. I am not!" retorted the slim gen-tleman, with great promptitude.

"Beg pardon, no offence! Volunteer, per-haps? Hair, you know, beard, et cætera, made me think you were in the military line. Many young gents now a-days are volunteers!"

"Mr. Sandham is an artist," said Mrs. Barford, interposing in dread lest there should be an outbreak.

"Oh ah!" said Mr. Mortiboy. "Bad trade that—demand not equal to supply, is it? Too many hands employed; barely bread and cheese, I'm told, for any but the top-sawyers."

"Sir!" said Mr. Sandham, in a loud tone of voice, and fiercely.

"Edward!" said Miss Kate, beneath her breath, appealingly.

"Won't you take some refreshment, Mr. Mortiboy?" asked Mrs. Barford, warningly. "We're just going to supper."

"No, thank you, mam," said Mr. Mortiboy. "I've a steak and potatoes waiting for me at the Royal, after which I shall turn it at once, as I'm done up by my journey. Good night, ladies all! Good night to you, sir! I'll look you up to-morrow morning, and if any of you want to go for a turn, I shall be proud to beau you about. Good night!" And beckoning his dog, Mr. Mortiboy took his departure.

Scarcely had the door closed behind him, than the long-restrained comments began.

"A pleasant visitor uncle Crump has sent us, mamma!" said Kate.

"Uncle Crump, indeed! Who never sent us anything before, except a five-pound note when poor papa died!" exclaimed Ellen.

"But you won't, will you, mamma, you won't be put upon in this way? You won't have this horrid man running in and out at all times and seasons, and——"

"And beau-ing us about! the vulgar wretch!" interrupted Kate.

"My dears! my dears!" said Mrs. Barford, "it strikes me that some one has been teaching you very strong language."

"Not I, Mrs. Barford," said Mr. Sandham; "absolve me from that; though I must own that if ever I saw a man who wanted kicking——"

"Nonsense, Mr. Sandham. This gentleman is imbued with certain London peculiarities, no doubt; but I dare say there's good in him. There must be, or he would never be the partner of such an upright man as Jonas Crump."

"Upright man! Pooh!" said Kate; and then the supper come in, and the subject dropped.

At nine o'clock next morning, just as the breakfast things had been cleared, and Mrs. Barford was going through her usual interview with the cook, Kate, who was sitting in the little bay-window, started and exclaimed: "Oh, mamma! Here's this horrid man!"

Ellen peeped over her shoulder and said, "I think he looks, if possible, more dreadful by day-light than by candlelight!"

Mr. John Mortiboy, utterly unconscious of the effect he was producing, unlatched the garden-gate, and then for the first time looking up, nodded shortly and familiarly at the sisters. "How do, young ladies?" he called from the garden. "Fine morning this: fresh and all that sort of thing! I feel better already. When a London man's a little overdone, nothing sets him up so soon as a sniff of the briny."

And then he took a great gulp, as if to swallow as much fresh air as possible, and entered the house, followed by his dog.

"Did you hear him, Nelly?" asked Kate. "The wretch! I'm sure I won't be seen walking with him, in his nasty black clothes, like an undertaker."

"He has a chimney-pot hat on, and has brought his umbrella! Fancy! At the sea!" said Ellen.

"Good morning, Mrs. Barford," said Mr. Mortiboy; "domestic arrangments, eh? I understand. If you've no objection, I'll do myself the pleasure of cutting my mutton with you to-day. And mutton it will be, I suppose! Can't get any beef here, I understand, except on Friday, which is killing-day for the barracks. Bad arrangement that; wants alteration."

"Hadn't you better alter it then, Mr. Mortiboy," said Kate; "superintending the butcher will be a pleasant way of spending your holiday."

"Joking miss, eh? Well I don't mind. But ain't you coming out, young ladies, for a mouthful of air. I suppose the old lady dont move so early."

"If you refer to mamma," said Ellen, frigidly, "she never goes out until just before dinner."

"Ah, I thought not. Old folks must wait until the air is what they call warmed by the sun. But that won't hinder our taking a turn, I suppose. Where's Whiskerandos?"

"If, as I presume, you meant Mr. Sandham the gentleman who was here last night, I cannot inform you Mr. Mortiboy," said Kate, with a very flushed face, and a slightly trembling voice; "but I would advise you not to let him hear you joking about him, as he is rather quick-tempered."

"Oh, indeed!" exclaimed Mr. Mortiboy, "a fire-eater is he? Well, there's no duelling now, you know. Any nonsense of that sort,—give a man in charge of a policeman, or summons him before a magistrate, and get him bound over."

Just at this moment Mrs. Barford came in and told the girls to get their hats on, and show Mr. Mortiboy the prettiest spots in the village, the Castle Hill, the ruined Abbey, and the Smuggler's Leap. To these places they went, Mr.

Mortiboy discoursing the whole way of the badness of the roads, and of what improvements might be made if they had a properly constituted local board of health at Penethly; declaring that the cries of "Milford oysters," and "fresh haddick," were entirely unconstitutional and illegal; as no one had a right to shout in the public streets; that there ought to be proper stands provided for the car-drivers; and that a regular police supervision was urgently demanded. He did not think much of the Abbey ruins, and he laughed in scorn at the story of the Smuggler's Leap. As they were on their homeward way, coming round the Castle Hill, they met Mr. Sandham, very ruddy and fresh, and shiny, and with a couple of towels in his hand. He took off his wide-awake as he approached the ladies, and bowed slightly to Mr. Mortiboy.

"Ah Mr. Sandham!" said Ellen, with an admonitory finger, you have been bathing again by St. Catherine's Rock, after all the warning we gave you!"

"My dear Ellen," interposed Kate with a petulent air, "how can you? If Mr. Sandham chooses to risk his life after what he has been told, it surely is nothing to us!"

"Now, Miss Kate, Miss Kate, that's not fair!" said Sandham; "you know," he added, dropping his voice, "that every word of yours would have weight with me, but the tide was slack this morning, and really there is no other place where a swimmer can really enjoy a bath. You are a swimmer, Mr. Mortiboy?"

"Yes, sir," replied that gentleman. "Yes, sir, I can manage it. I've had lessons at Peerless Pool and the Hulborn Baths, and can keep up well enough. But I don't like it. I dont see much fun in what are absurdly called the 'manly exercises.' Twenty years ago, young men used to like driving coaches; now I can't conceive duller work than holding a bunch of thick leather reins in your hand, steering four tired horses, sitting on a hard seat, and listening to the conversation of an uneducated coachman. I never ride, because I hate bumping up and down on a hard saddle and rubbing the skin off my body; I never play cricket, because in the hot weather I like to keep quiet and cool, and not toil in the sun; and as to going out shooting and stumping over miles of stubble in September, lugging a big gun and tiring myself to death, I look upon that as the pursuit of a maniac! I am a practical man!"

"You are indeed!" said Kate, as she dropped gradually behind with Mr. Sandham, and left the practical man and her sister Ellen to lead the way to the house.

It is unnecessary to recount the sayings and doings of Mr. John Mortiboy during the next few days. It is enough that he spent the greater portion of them with the Barford family, and that he so elaborated his ideas of practicality, and so enveighed against every thing that was not absolutely useful in a mercantile point of view—including, in a measure, art, poetry, music, and the domestic affections—that he incurred the unmitigated hatred of the young ladies, and even fell to zero in Mrs. Barford's estimation.

It was about the fifth morning after the intrusion of this utterly incongruous element into the society of Albion Villa, that Ellen and Kate strolled out immediately after breakfast with the view of escaping the expected visit of their persecutor, and made their way to the Castle Hill. The night had been tempestuous, and from their window they had noticed that a heavy sea was running: they consequently were not surprised to see a little group of people gathered on the heights looking towards St. Catherine's Rock: a huge mass of granite surmounted by an old ruin, round which, when it was insulated at high water, the tide always swept with a peculiar and dangerous swirl. But when they joined the group, among which were several of their friends, they found that the concourse were regarding, with interest mingled with fright, the movements of a swimmer who had rounded the extremity of Catherine's, and was seen making for the shore.

"He'll never do it," said Captain Calthorp, an old half-pay dragoon, who had been tempted by the cheapness of Penethly to pitch his tent there; "he'll never do it, by Jove! Yes! Well struggled, sir; he made a point there—hold on, now, and he's in."

"Who is it? asked the coast-guard lieutenant who was standing by. "Any one we know?"

"I can't tell at this distance!" said Captain Calthorp, "though it looks like—stay! There's one of your look-out men on the height, with a glass; give him a hail!"

"Yoho! Morgan!" cried the lieutenant. "Ay, ay, sir!" was the man's ready response, though the glass was never moved. "Bring that glass down here!" "Ay, ay, sir;" and in two minutes the old coast-guard man was by his officer's side. He saluted and handed the glass, but as he did so he said, in an undertone, "God help the gentleman, he's done! Ah, look you now, poor thing, nothing can save him."

"What!" cries the lieutenant, clapping the glass to his eye. "By Jove, you're right! he's in a bad way, and it—why it's the artist chap, that friend of the Barfords'!"

"Who?" screamed Kate, rushing up at the moment. "Who did you say, Mr. Lawford? Oh, for God's sake, save him! Save him, Mr. Lawford! Save him, Captain Calthorp!"

"My dear young lady," said the last-named gentleman, "I am sure Lawford did'nt know you were here, or he wouldn't——"

"This is no time for ceremony, Captain Calthorp," said Ellen; "for Heaven's sake let some effort be made to save my sister's——to save Mr. Sandham!"

"My dear Miss Barford," said Lawford, who had been whispering with Morgan, "I fear no mortal aid can avail the poor dear fellow now. Before we could descend the rock, and launch a boat, with the tide ebbing at the rate it now is——"

"Hur would have been swep' round Catherine's, and away out to sea!" said Morgan.

"Oh, help him!" screamed Kate. "Oh, how cruel! how cowardly! Oh, help him, Mr Lawford!" She lifted up her hands piteously to the lieutenant. "Oh, Mr. Mortiboy'" she exclaimed, as that gentleman came slowly sauntering up the hill with Beppo at his heels, "for God's sake, save Mr. Sandham!"

"Save—Mr. Sandham—my dear young lady; I don't exactly comprehend!" began Mr. Mortiboy, looking vaguely in the direction of her outstretched hand: then suddenly, "Good Lord! is that his head? There! Down there!"

"Yes!" whispered Ellen Barford; "yes! They say he will be whirled away before a boat could be launched—they say he is lost now!"

"Not at all! Not yet, at least!" replied Mortiboy, excited, but without much perceptible alteration of manner. "While there's life there's hope, you know, Miss B., and even yet we may—Here, Beppo! Hi, man! hi! Good boy!" The dog came, leaping round his master. "Hi! ho! Not here! There! there! Look, boy!" catching him by the collar, and pointing down to where Sandham's head was a mere speck on the water. "Look, man! Look, old boy! He sees it, by Jove!" as the dog uttered a low growl, and became restive. "In, old man! In, fine fellow! In, Beppo! Look! Noble dog, in he goes!"

In he went, with one bound over the low stone wall, then quickly down the sloping slippery boulders, then with a plunge into the sea—lost sight of for a moment, rising to view again, paddling off straight for the drowning man. The swift current whirled him in eddies here and there, but still the brave dog persevered; the spectators held their breath, as they saw him bearing down upon the black speck, which was every second growing smaller and smaller, and receding further and further from the land. But the dog made grand progress, the strong sucking undercurrent helped him, and he arrived at Sandham's

side just in time for the drowning man to fling his arms round the dog's neck, and to feel his shoulder seized by the dog's teeth. They saw this from the shore, and then Kate ' Barford fainted.

But the work was only half done : the dog turned round and battled bravely for the shore, but he was encumbered by his burden, and now the current was against him. He strove and strove, but the way he made was small, and every foot was gained with intense struggling and exertion. "By Jove! He'll never do it," cried Lieutenant Lawford, with the glass at his eye, and, as he said the words, old Morgan, the preventive man, added through his teeth, "Hur must be helped, at any cost," and sped away down the rock, shaping his course to where a small pleasure-boat lay high and dry on the sand. "I'm with you, governor," cried John Mortiboy; "I can't feather, but I pull a strongish oar;" and he followed the old man as best he could. The boat was reached, and pushed by main force to the water's edge, where Mortiboy entered it, and old Morgan ran in, waist-deep, to give it the starting shove, and leaped in to join his comrade. On they pulled, Morgan with a measured steady stroke, Mortiboy with fevered strong jerks that sent the boat's head now to the right, now to the left : when old Morgan, suddenly looking over his shoulder, called out "Hur's done! Hur's sinking now, both on 'em!" Mortiboy looked round too; they were still some ten boats' length from the object of their pursuit, and both dog and man were vanishing. "Not yet!" cried he; and in an instant he had torn off the black coat and the Wellington boots, and had flung himself, as nobly as his own dog, into the sea.

A very few strokes brought him to Sandham : he seized him by the hair of his head, and battled bravely with the waves; the dog, recognising his master, seemed to take fresh courage, and the trio floated until old Morgan dragged them one by one into the boat. When they reached the shore, all Peucthly was on the beach, cheering with all its might : they lifted out Mr. Sandham, insensible but likely to recover, and they administered a very stiff glass of grog to Mr. Mortiboy, who was shivering like an aspen-leaf, but who received even greater warmth from a warm pressure of Ellen Barford's hand, and a whispered "God bless you, Mr. Mortiboy!" than from the grog—though he took that, too, like a man whom it comforted. As for Beppo, I don't know what the fishing population would not have done for him, but that he positively refused to stir from Sandham's side. As they carried the artist up to his lodgings the dog buried his nose in the pendent hand, and did not leave until he had seen his charge safely placed in bed.

Mr. Sandham was, in his own words, "All right" next day; but Mr. Mortiboy, unaccustomed to exercise and damp, fell ill, and was confined to his bed for several weeks—would have never left it, I think, but for the care and attention of his three nurses from Albion Villa. Of these, Ellen was the most constant and the most regular, and the patient always seemed better under her care.

"He is making progress, Kate," she said one night to her sister. "He his a good patient. You know, as he would say himself, he is so practical!"

"God bless his practicality, Nell," said Kate, with tears in her eyes. "Think what it did for us!"

Three years have passed since then, Major. and a family group is going to be gathered in a large square room built as a kind of excrescence to a very pretty villa in Kensington. This is to be the studio of Mr. Sandham, A. R. A. But as the mortar and plaster are extraordinarily slow in drying (when where they not, Major?), Mr. Sandham, A. R. A., come up from Wales with the family group to take possession as established the group at the excellent Lodgings of the excellent Mrs. Lirriper, and he, the owner of said studio, is smoking a pipe with a worthy Major, and smoothing with' his slippered foot the rough curly back of his dog Beppo, who is stretched in front of the fire. Mrs. Sandham, formerly Kate Barford, is working at a baby's frock, and asking now and then the advice of her sister, who is frilling a little cap. (There they are, Major. Don't tell them that I said so.)

"How late John is to-night, Ellen!" said old Mrs. Barford, from her place in the chimney-corner. (You hear her, Major?)

"Always at Christmas-time, dear mother," says Ellen. (There she is, Major,) "Since uncle Crump's death, you know, John's business is trebled, and it all hangs on him, dear old fellow!"

"He will be late for supper, Nelly," says Sandham. "(—Excuse me. Major.)"

"No, he won't, Ned!" cries a cheery voice at the door as John Mortiboy appears; "no he won't. He's never late for any thing good Don't you know, he's a practical man ?"

—Mr. Mortiboy. Major Jackmann, Major, Mr. Mortiboy ?

V.

HOW THE THIRD FLOOR KNEW THE POTTERIES.

I AM a plain man, Major, and you may not dislike to hear a plain statement of facts from me. Some of those facts lie beyond my understanding.

I do not pretend to explain them. I only know that they happened as I relate them, and that I pledge myself for the truth of every word of them.

I began life roughly enough, down among the Potteries. I was an orphan ; and my earliest recollections are of a great porcelain manufactory in the country of the Potteries, where I helped about the yard, picked up what halfpence fell in my way, and slept in a harness-loft over the stable. Those were hard times ; but things bettered themselves as I grew older and stronger, especially after George Barnard had come to be foreman of the yard.

George Barnard was a Wesleyan—we were mostly dissenters in the Potteries—sober, clear-headed, somewhat sulky and silent, but a good fellow every inch of him, and my best friend at the time when I most needed a good friend. He took me out of the yard, and set me to the furnace-work. He entered me on the book at a fixed rate of wages. He helped me to pay for a little cheap schooling four nights a week ; and he led me to go with him on Sundays to the chapel down by the river-side, where I first saw Leah Payne. She was his sweetheart, and so pretty that I used to forget the preacher and every body else, when I looked at her. When she joined in the singing, I heard no voice but hers. If she asked me for the hymn-book, I used to blush and tremble. I believe I worshipped her, in my stupid ignorant way; and I think I worshipped Barnard almost as blindly, though after a different passion. I felt I owed him every thing. I knew that he had saved me, body and mind ; and I looked up to him as a savage might look up to a missionary.

Leah was the daughter of a plumber, who lived close by the chapel. She was twenty, and George about seven or eight-and-thirty. Some captious folks said there was too much difference in their ages ; but she was so serious-minded, and they loved each other so earnestly and quietly, that if nothing had come between them during their courtship, I don't believe the question of disparity would ever have troubled the happiness of their married lives. Something did come, however ; and that something was a Frenchman, called Louis Laroche. He was a painter on porcelain, from the famous works at Sèvres: and our master, it was said, had engaged him for three years certain, at such wages as none of our own people, however skilful, could hope to command. It was about the beginning or middle of September when he first came among us. He looked very young ; was small, dark, and well made; had little white soft hands, and a silky moustache ; and spoke English nearly as well as I do. None of us liked him ; but that was only natural, seeing how he was put over the head of every English-

man in the place. Besides, though he was always smiling and civil, we couldn't help seeing
that he thought himself ever so much better than
the rest of us; and that was not pleasant. Neither
was it pleasant to see him strolling about the
town, dressed just like a gentleman, when working hours were over; smoking good cigars, when
we were forced to be content with a pipe of common tobacco; hiring a horse on Sunday after-
noons, when we were trudging a-foot; and taking his pleasure as if the world was made for him
to enjoy, and us to work in.

"Ben, boy," said George, "there's something
wrong about that Frenchman."

It was on a Saturday afternoon, and we were
sitting on a pile of empty seggars against the
door of the furnace-room, waiting till the men
should all have cleared out of the yard. Seggars
are deep earthen boxes in which the pottery is
put, while being fired in the kiln.

I looked up, inquiringly.

"About the Count?" said I, for that was the
nickname by which he went in the pottery.

George nodded, and paused for a moment with
his chin resting on his palms.

"He has an evil eye," said he; "and a false
smile. Something wrong about him."

I drew nearer, and listened to George as if he
had been an oracle.

"Besides," added he, in his slow quiet way,
with his eyes fixed straight-before him as if he
was thinking aloud, "there's a young look about
him that isn't natural; Take him just at sight,
and you'd think he was almost a boy; but look
close at him—see the little fine wrinkles under
his eyes, and the hard lines about his mouth, and
then tell me his age, if you can! Why, Ben, boy,
he's as old as I am, pretty near: ay, and as strong
too. You stare; but I tell you that, slight as he
looks, he could fling you over his shoulder as if
you were a feather. And as for his hands, little
and white as they are, there are muscles of iron
inside them, take my word for it."

"But, George, how can you know?"

"Because I have a warning against him," replied George, very gravely. "Because, whenever
he is by, I feel as if my eyes saw clearer, and my
ears heard keener, than at other times. May be
it's presumption, but I sometimes feel as if I had
a call to guard myself and others against him.
Look at the children, Ben, how they shrink away
from him; and see there, now! Ask Captain
what he thinks of him! Ben, that dog likes him
no better than I do."

I looked, and saw Captain crouching by his
kennel with his ears laid back, growling audibly,
as the Frenchman came slowly down the steps
leading from his own workshop at the upper end

of the yard. On the last step he paused; lighted
a cigar; glanced round, as if to see whether any
one was by; and then walked straight over to
within a couple of yards of the kennel. Captain
gave a short angry snarl, and laid his muzzle
close down upon his paws, ready for a spring.
The Frenchman folded his arms deliberately,
fixed his eyes on the dog, and stood calmly smoking. He knew exactly how far he dared go, and
kept just that one foot out of harm's way. All
at once he stooped, puffed a mouthful of smoke
in the dog's eyes, burst into a mocking laugh,
turned lightly on his heel, and walked away:
leaving Captain straining at his chain, and bark-
ing after him like a mad creature.

Days went by, and I, at work in my own de-
partment, saw no more of the Count. Sunday
came—the third, I think, after I had talked with
George in the yard. Going with George to chapel, as usual, in the morning, I noticed that there
was something strange and anxious in his face,
and that he scarcely opened his lips to me on the
way. Still I said nothing. It was not my place to
question him: and I remember thinking to myself that the cloud would all clear off as soon as he
found himself by Leah's side, holding the same
book, and joining in the same hymn. It did not,
however, for no Leah was there, I looked every
moment at the door, expecting to see her sweet
face coming in; but George never lifted his eyes
from his book, or seemed to notice that her place
was empty. Thus the whole service went by, and
my thoughts wandered continually from the words
of the preacher. As soon as the last blessing was
spoken, and we were fairly across the threshold, I
turned to George and asked if Leah was ill?

"No," said he gloomily. "She's not ill."

"Then why wasn't she—?"

"I'll tell you why," he interrupted impatiently.
"Because you've seen her here for the last time.
She's never coming to chapel again."

"Never coming to the chapel again?" I fal-
tered, laying my hand on his sleeve in the earn-
estness of my surprise. "Why, George, what is
the matter?"

But he shook my hand off, and stamped with
his iron heel till the pavement rang again.

"Don't ask me," said he, roughly. "Let me
alone. You'll know soon enough."

And with this he turned off down a by-lane
leading towards the hills, and left me without
another word.

I had had plenty of hard treatment in my time;
but never, until that moment, an angry look or
syllable for George. I did not know how to bear
it. That day my dinner seemed as if it would
choke me; and in the afternoon I went out and
wandered restlessly about the fields till the hour

for evening prayers came round I then returned to the chapel, and sat down on a tomb outside, waiting for George. I saw the congregation go in by twos and threes. I heard the first psalm-tune echo solemnly through the evening stillness; but no George came. Then the service began, and I knew that, punctual as his habits were, it was of no use to expect him any longer. Where could he be? What could have happened? Why should Leah Payne never come to chapel again? Had she gone over to some other sect, and was that why George seemed so unhappy?

Sitting there in the little dreary churchyard with the darkness fast gathering around me, I asked myself these questions over and over again, till my brain ached; for I was not much used to thinking about anything in those times. At last, I could bear to sit quiet no longer. The sudden thought struck me that I would go to Leah, and learn what the matter was, from her own lips. I sprang to my feet, and set off at once towards her home.

It was quite dark, and a light rain was beginning to fall. I found the garden-gate open, and a quick hope flashed across me that George might be there. I drew back for a moment, hesitating whether to knock or ring, when a sound of voices in the passage, and the sudden gleaming of a bright line of light under the door, warned me that some one was coming out. Taken by surprise, and quite unprepared for the moment with anything to say, I shrank back behind the porch, and waited until those within should have passed out. The door opened, and the light streamed suddenly upon the rose and the white gravel.

"It rains," said Leah, bending forward and shading the candle with her hand.

"And is as cold as Siberia," added another voice, which was not George's, and yet sounded strangely familiar. "Ugh! what a climate for such a flower as my darling to bloom in!"

"Is it so much finer in France?" asked Leah, softly.

"As much finer as blue skies and sunshine can make it. Why, my angel, even your bright eyes will be ten times brighter, and your rosy cheeks ten times rosier, when they are transplanted to Paris. Ah! I can give you no idea of the wonders of Paris—the broad streets planted with trees, the palaces, the shops, the gardens?—it is a city of enchantment."

"It must be, indeed!" said Leah. And you will really take me to see all those beautiful shops?"

"Every Sunday, my darling—Bah! don't look so shocked. The shops in Paris are always open on Sunday, and everybody makes holiday. You will soon get over these prejudices."

"I fear it is very wrong to take so much pleasure in the things of this world," sighed Leah.

The Frenchman laughed and answered her with a kiss.

"Good night, my sweet little saint!" and he ran lightly down the path, and disappeared in the darkness. Leah sighed again, lingered a moment, and then closed the door.

Stupified and bewildered, I stood for some seconds like a stone statue, unable to move; scarcely able to think. At length, I roused myself, as it were mechanically, and went towards the gate. At that instant a heavy hand was laid upon my shoulder, and a hoarse voice close beside my ear, said :

"Who are you? What are you doing here?"

It was George. I knew him at once, in spite of the darkness, and stammered his name. He took his hand quietly from my shoulder.

"How long have you been here? said he, fiercely. "What right have you to lurk about, like a spy in the dark? God help me, Ben—I'm half mad. I don't mean to be harsh to you."

"I'm sure you don't," I cried, earnestly.

"It's that cursed Frenchman," he went on, in a voice that sounded like the groan of one in pain. "He's a villain. I know he's a villain ; and I've had a warning against him ever since the first moment he came among us. He'll make her miserable, and break her heart some day—my pretty Leah—and I loved her so! But I'll be revenged—as sure as there's a sun in heaven, I'll be revenged!"

His vehemence terrified me. I tried to persuade him to go home ; but he would not listen to me.

"No, no," he said. "Go home yourself, boy, and let me be. My blood is on fire : this rain is good for me."

"If I could only do something to help you——"

"You can't," interrupted he. "Nobody can help me. I'm a ruined man, and I don't care what becomes of me. The Lord forgive me! my heart is full of wickedness, and my thoughts are the promptings of Satan. There go—for Heaven's sake, go. I don't know what I say, or what I do!"

I went, for I did not dare refuse any longer ; but I lingered a while at the corner of the street, and watched him pacing to and fro, to and fro in the driving rain. At length I turned reluctantly away, and went home.

I lay awake that night for hours, thinking over the events of the day, and hating the Frenchman from my very soul. I could not hate Leah. I had worshipped her too long and too faithfully for that; but I looked upon her as a creature given over to destruction. I fell asleep towards morning, and woke again shortly after daybreak. When I reached the pottery, I found George there before me, looking very pale, but quite himself, and setting the men to their work the same as usual. I said nothing about what had happened the day before. Something in his face silenced me; but seeing him so steady and composed, I took heart and began to hope he had fought through the worst of his trouble. By-and-by the Frenchman came through the yard, gay and off-hand, with his cigar in his mouth, and his hands in his pockets. George turned sharply away into one of the workshops, and shut the door. I drew a deep breath of relief. My dread was to see them come to an open quarrel; and I made up my mind never to breathe another syllable on the subject, unless he began.

Wednesday came. I had overslept myself that morning, and came to work a quarter after the hour, expecting to be fined; for George was very strict as foreman of the yard, and treated friends and enemies just the same. Instead of blaming me, however, he called me up, and said:

"Ben, whose turn is it this week to sit up?"

"Mine, sir," I replied. (I always called him "Sir" in working hours.)

"Well, then, you may go home to-day, and the same on Thursday and Friday; for there's a large batch of work for the ovens to-night, and there'll be the same to-morrow night and the night after."

"All right, sir," said I. "Then I'll be here by seven this evening."

"No, half-past nine will be soon enough. I've some accounts to make up, and I shall be here myself till then. Mind you are true to time, though."

"I'll be as true as the clock, sir," I replied, and was turning away when he called me back again.

"You're a good lad, Ben," said he. Shake hands."

I seized his hand, and pressed it warmly.

"If I'm good for anything, George," I answered with all my heart, "it's you who have made me so. God bless you for it!"

"Amen!" said he, in a troubled voice, putting his hand to his hat.

And so we parted.

In general, I went to bed by day when I was attending to the firing by night; but this morning I had already slept longer than usual, and wanted exercise more than rest. So I ran home; put a bit of bread and meat in my pocket; snatched up my big thorn stick; and started off for a long day in the country. When I came home, it was quite dark and beginning to rain, just as it had begun to rain at about the same time that v retched Sunday evening: so I changed my wet

boots, had an early supper and a nap in the chimney-corner, and went down to the works at a few minutes before half-past nine. Arriving at the factory gate, I found it ajar, and so walked in and closed it after me. I remember thinking at the time that it was unlike George's usual caution to leave it so: but it passed from my mind next moment. Having slipped in the bolt, I then went straight over to George's little counting-house, where the gas was shining cheerfully in the window. Here also, somewhat to my surprise, I found the door open, and the room empty. I went in. The threshold and part of the floor was wetted by the driving rain. The wages-book was open on the desk, George's pen stood in the ink, and his hat hung on its usual peg in the corner. I concluded, of course, that he had gone round to the ovens, so following him, I took down his hat and carried it with me, for it was now raining fast.

The baking-houses lay just opposite, on the other side of the yard. There were three of them, opening one out of the other; and in each, the great furnace filled all the middle of the room. These furnaces are, in fact, large kilns built of brick, with an oven closed in by an iron door in the centre of each, and a chimney going up through the roof. The pottery, enclosed in seggars, stands round inside on shelves, and has to be turned from time to time while the firing is going on. To turn these seggars, test the heat, and keep the fire up, was my work at the period of which I am now telling you, Major.

Well! I went through the baking-houses one after the other, and found all empty alike. Then a strange vague uneasy feeling came over me, and I began to wonder what could have become of George. It was possible that he might be in one of the workshops; so I ran over to the counting-house, lighted a lantern, and made a thorough survey of the yards. I tried the doors; they were all locked as usual. I peeped into the open sheds; they were all vacant. I called "George! George!" in every part of the outer premises; but the wind and rain drove back my voice, and no other voice replied to it. Forced at last to believe that he was really gone, I took his hat back to the counting-house, put away the wages-book, extinguished the gas, and prepared for my solitary watch.

The night was mild, and the heat in the baking-rooms intense. I knew, by experience, that the ovens had been overheated, and that none of the porcelain must go in at least for the next two hours: so I carried my stool to the door, settled myself in a sheltered corner where the air could reach me, but not the rain, and fell to wondering where George could have gone, and why he should not have waited till the time appointed. That he had left in haste was clear—not because his hat remained behind, for he might have had a cap with him—but because he had left the book open, and the gas lighted. Perhaps one of the workmen had met with some accident, and he had been summoned away so urgently that he had no time to think of anything; perhaps he would even now come back presently to see that all was right before he went home to his lodgings. Turning these things over in my mind, I grew drowsy, my thoughts wandered, and I fell asleep.

I cannot tell how long my nap lasted. I had walked a great distance that day, and I slept heavily; but I awoke all in a moment, with a sort of terror upon me, and, looking up, saw George Barnard sitting on a stool before the oven door, with the firelight full upon his face.

Ashamed to be found sleeping, I started to my feet. At the same instant, he rose, turned away without even looking towards me, and went out into the next room.

"Don't be angry, George," I cried, following him. "None of the seggars are in. I knew the fires were too strong, and——"

The words died on my lips. I had followed him from the first room to the second, from the second to the third, and in the third—I lost him.

I could not believe my eyes. I opened the end door leading into the yard, and looked out; but he was no where in sight. I went round to the back of the baking-houses, looked behind the furnaces, ran over to the counting-house, called him by his name over and over again; but all was dark, silent, lonely, as ever.

Then I remembered how I had bolted the outer gate, and how impossible it was that he should have come in without ringing. Then, too, I began again to doubt the evidence of my own senses, and to think I must have been dreaming.

I went back to my old post by the door of the first baking-house, and sat down for a moment to collect my thoughts.

"In the first place," said I to myself, "there is but one outer gate. That outer gate I bolted on the inside, and it is bolted still. In the next place, I searched the premises, and found all the sheds empty, and the workshop-doors padlocked as usual on the outside. I proved that George was nowhere about, when I came, and I knew he could not have come in since, without my knowledge. Therefore it is a dream. It is certainly a dream, and there's an end of it."

And with this I trimmed my lantern and proceeded to test the temperature of the furnaces. We used to do this, I should tell you, by the introduction of little roughly-moulded lumps of common fire-clay. If the heat is too great, they

crack; if too little, they remain damp and moist; if just right, they become firm and smooth all over, and pass into the biscuit stage. Well, I took my three little lumps of clay, put one in each oven, waited while I counted five hundred, and then went round again to see the results. The two first were in capital condition, the third had flown into a dozen pieces. This proved that the seggars might at once go into ovens One and Two, but that number Three had been overheated, and must be allowed to go on cooling for an hour or two longer.

I therefore stocked One and Two with nine rows of seggars, three deep on each shelf; left the rest waiting till number Three was in a condition to be trusted; and, fearful of falling asleep again, now that the firing was in progress, walked up and down the rooms to keep myself awake. This was hot work, however, and I could not stand it very long; so I went back presently to my stool by the door, and fell to thinking about my dream. The more I thought of it, the more strangely real it seemed, and the more I felt convinced that I was actually on my feet, when I saw George get up and walk into the adjoining room. I was also certain that I had still continued to see him as he passed out of the second room into the third, and that at that time I was even following his very footsteps. Was it possible, I asked myself, that I could have been up and moving, and yet not quite awake? I had heard of people walking in their sleep. Could it be that I was walking in mine, and never waked till I reached the cool air of the yard? All this seemed likely enough, so I dismissed the matter from my mind, and passed the rest of the night in attending to the seggars, adding fresh fuel from time to time to the furnaces of the first and second ovens, and now and then taking a turn through the yards. As for Number Three, it kept up its heat to such a degree that it was almost day before I dared trust the seggars to go in it.

Thus the hours went by; and at half-past seven on Thursday morning, the men came to their work. It was now my turn to go off duty, but I wanted to see George before I left, and so waited for him in the counting-house, while a lad named Steve Storr took my place at the ovens. But the clock went on from half-past seven to a quarter to eight; then to eight o'clock; then to a quarter-past eight—and still George never made his appearance. At length, when the hand got round to half-past eight, I grew weary of waiting, took up my hat, ran home, went to bed, and slept profoundly until past four in the afternoon.

That evening I went down to the factory quite early; for I had a restlessness upon me, and I wanted to see George before he left for the night. This time I found the gate bolted, and I rang for admittance.

"How early you are, Ben!" said Steve Storr, as he let me in.

"Mr. Barnard's not gone?" I asked quickly, for I saw at the first glance that the gas was out in the counting-house.

"He's not gone," said Steve, "because he's never been."

"Never been?"

"No; and what's stranger still, he's not been home, since dinner yesterday."

"But he was here last night?"

"Oh yes, he was here last night, making up the books. John Parker was with him till past six; and you found him here, didn't you, at half past nine?"

I shook my head.

"Well, he's gone, anyhow. Good night!"

"Good night!"

I took the lantern from his hand, bolted him out mechanically, and made my way to the baking-houses like one in a stupor. George gone? Gone without a word of warning to his employer, or of farewell to his fellow-workmen? I could not understand it. I could not believe it. I sat down bewildered, incredulous, stunned. Then come hot tears, doubts, terrifying suspicions. I remembered the wild words he had spoken a few nights back; the strange calm by which they were followed; my dream of the evening before. I had heard of men who drowned themselves for love; and the turbid Severn ran close by—so close, that one might pitch a stone into it from some of the workshop windows.

These thoughts were too terrible. I dared not dwell upon them. I turned to work, to free myself from them, if I could ; and began by examining the ovens. The temperature of all was much higher than on the previous night, the heat having been gradually increased during the last twelve hours. It was now my business to keep the heat on the increase for twelve more ; after which it would be allowed, as gradually, to subside, until the pottery was cool enough for removal. To turn the seggars, and add fuel to the two first furnaces, was my first work. As before, I found number three in advance of the others, and so left it for half an hour, or an hour. I then went round the yard; tried the doors; let the dog loose; and brought him back with me to the baking-houses, for company. After that I set my lantern on a shelf beside the door, took a book from my pocket, and began to read.

I remember the title of the book as well as possible. It was called Bowlker's Art of Angling,

and contained little rude cuts of all kinds of artificial flies, hooks and other tackle. But I could not keep my mind to it for two minutes together; and at last I gave it up in despair, covered my face with my hands, and fell into a long absorbing painful train of thought. A considerable time had gone by thus—may be an hour—when I was roused by a low whimpering howl from Captain, who was lying at my feet. I looked up with a start, just as I had started the night before, and with the same vague terror ; and saw, exactly in the same place and in the same attitude, with the firelight full upon him—George Barnard !

At this sight, a fear heavier than the fear of death fell upon me, and my tongue seemed paralysed in my mouth. Then, just as last night, I rose, or seemed to rise, and went slowly out into the next room. A power stronger than myself appeared to compel me, reluctantly, to follow him. I saw him pass through the second room—cross the threshold of the third room—walk straight up to the oven—and there pause. He then turned, for the first time, with the glare of the red firelight pouring out upon him from the open door of the furnace, and looked at me, face to face. In the same instant his whole frame and countenance seemed to glow and become transparent, as if the fire were all within him—and in that glow he became, as it were, absorbed into the furnace, and disappeared.

I uttered a wild cry, tried to stagger from the room, and fell insensible before I reached the door.

When I next opened my eyes the gray dawn was in the sky ; the furnace doors were all closed as I had left them when I last went round; the dog was quietly sleeping not far from my side ; and the men were ringing at the gate, to be let in.

I told my tale from beginning to end, and was laughed at, as a matter of course, by all who heard it. When it was found, however, that my statement never varied, and, above all, that George Barnard continued absent, some few began to talk it over seriously, and among those few the master of the works. He forbade the furnace to be cleared out, called in the aid of a celebrated naturalist, and had the ashes submitted to a scientific examination. The result was as follows:

The ashes were found to have been largely saturated with some kind of fatty animal matter. A considerable portion of those ashes consisted of charred bone. A semi-circular piece of iron which evidently had once been the heel of a workman's heavy boot, was found, half fused, at one corner of the furnace. Near it a tibia bone which still retained sufficient of its original form and textture to render identification possible

This bone, however, was so much charred, that it fell into powder on being handled.

After this, not many doubted that George Barnard had been foully murdered, and that his body had been trust into the furnace. Suspicion fell upon Louis Laroche. He was arrested, a coroner's inquest was held, and every circumstance connected with the night of the murder was as thoroughly sifted and investigated as possible. All the sifting in the world, however, failed either to clear or to condemn Louis Laroche. On the very night of his release he left the place by the mail train, and was never seen or heard of there again. As for Leah, I know not what became of her. I went away myself before many weeks were over, and never have set foot among the Potteries from that hour to this.

VI.

HOW THE BEST ATTIC WAS UNDER A CLOUD.

MAJOR, you have assured me of your sympathy; you shall receive my confidence. I not only seem—as you have searchingly observed—"under a cloud," but I am. I entered (shall I say like a balloon?) into a dense stratum of cloud, obscuring the wretched earth from view, in the year eighteen hundred and dash, in the sweet summer season, when nature, as has been remarked by some distinguished poet, puts on her gayest garb, and when her countenance is adorned with the sunniest and loveliest of smiles. Ah! what are now those smiles to me? What care I for sunshine or for verdure? For me, summer is no more. For, I must ever remember that it was in the summer that canker ate its way into my heart's core—that it was in the summer that I parted with my belief in mankind—that it was in summer that I knew for the first time that WOMAN—but this is premature. Pray be seated.

I have no doubt that my appearance and words convey to you, Major, and to all observant persons, that I have an elevated soul. In fact, were it otherwise, how could I be under a cloud? The sordid soul won't blight. To one possessing an elevated soul like myself, the task of keeping accounts at a ferrier's (in a large way) could not be otherwise than repugnant. It was repugnant, and the rapture of getting a holiday, which was annually accorded me in June—not a busy month in the fur-trade—was something perfectly indescribable. Of course, whenever my vacation time came round, I invariably rushed off to the country; there to indulge my natural tastes and commune with our mother, Nature.

On the particular occasion of which I have now to speak, I had, however, other commonings to look forward to, besides those in which nature takes her silent yet eloquent part. I loved—Aha!

—Love—Woman—Vertigo—Despair—I beg your pardon—I will be calm. I loved Miss Nuttlebury. Miss Nuttlebury lived in the neighbourhood of Dartford (at a convenient distance from the Powder-Mills), so in the neighbourhood of Dartford (rather further from the Powder-Mills) I determined to spend my vacation. I made arrangements at a certain small roadside inn for my board and lodging.

I was acquainted—nay, I was on friendly terms with the Nuttleburys. Mr. Nuttlebury, a land surveyor in a rather small way, was an old friend of my father's; so I had access to the house. I had access also, as I thought, to the heart of Mary, which was Miss Nuttlebury's name. If I was mistaken—Aha!—but I am again premature. You are aware, or perhaps you are not aware, that my name is Oliver Cromwell Shrubsole—so called after the great Protector of British rights; the man who, or rather but for whom—but I am again premature, or, rather, I should say, on the whole the reverse.

The first days of my residence near Fordleigh, the name of the village where the Nuttleburys dwelt, were happy in the extreme. I saw much of Mary. I walked with Mary, made hay with Mary, observed the moon in Mary's society, and in vain sought to interest Mary in those mysterious shadows which diversify the surface of that luminary. I subsequently endeavoured to interest the fair girl in other matters nearer home—in short, in myself; and I fondly imagined that I succeeded in doing so.

One day, when I had dropped in at the family dinner-hour—not from base motives, for I was boarded at my inn by contract—I found the family conversing on a subject which caused me considerable uneasiness. At the moment of my arrival, Mr. Nuttlebury was uttering these words:

"At what time will he be here, then?" (He?)

I listened breathless, after the first salutation had passed, for more; I was not long in ascertaining that "he" was a cousin of Mary's, who was coming down to spend some days at Fordleigh, and whose arrival was anticipated by the whole family with expressions of delight. The younger boy and girl Nuttleburys seemed to be especially rapturous at the prospect of the Beast's arrival, and from this I augured ill. Altogether, I felt that there was a trying scene coming; that my opportunities of converse with my soul's idol would be fewer than they had been, and that general discomfort and misery were about to ensue. I was right.

Oho!—I beg your pardon—I will be calm.

The Beast, "He," arrived in the course of that very afternoon, and I believe I am not speaking too strongly in affirming that we—"he" and I—hated each other cordially from the first moment of our exchanged glances. He was an underhand looking beast, short of stature; such a creature as any high-souled woman should have abhorred the sight of; but his prospects were good, he having some small situation in the Customhouse, on the strength of which he gave himself airs, as if he was a member of the government; and when he talked of the country, he spoke of it as "we." Alas! how could I compete with him? What could I talk about, except the fur-trade, and the best method of keeping the moths under? So, having nothing to talk about, I remained sulky and glum and silent; a condition in which a man does not usually tell to advantage in society. I felt that I was not telling to advantage, and this made me hate the beast—whose disgusting name was Huffell—more cordially than before. It affords me a gloomy pleasure to think that I never once lost an opportunity of contradicting him—flat—in the course of that first evening. But, somehow or other, he generally got the best of it; possibly because I had contradicted him for the sake of doing so, and without bestowing a thought upon the rights or wrongs of the matter under discussion. But the worst of it was, that it did appear to me that Mary—my Mary—seemed to be on the side of Huffell. Her eyes would brighten—or I thought so—when he triumphed. And what right had she to go and fig herself out like that, in all her finery for Huffell? She never did so for me.

"This must be put a stop to, and promptly," I muttered to myself, as I walked back to my inn in a state of the most intense fury. And to leave him there with the field all to himself! What might he not be saying of me at the moment? Turning me into ridicule, perhaps? I resolved to crush him next day, or perish in the attempt.

Next day I lay in wait for him, and presently I thought my opportunity had come.

"We shall have to make some change about that appointment of Sir Cornelius," said Huffell, "or he'll have all his family in the office in a week."

"What do you mean by we?" I asked, with ferocious emphasis.

"I mean government," he answerred, cooly.

"Well but you're not government," was my dignified reply. "The Custom house, even as represented by those who hold high positions in it, has as little to do with governing the country as can well be imagined. The higher officers in the Custom-house are at best rather government servants than government advisers, while the lower—"

"Well sir, 'the lower?'"

"The less they try to connect themselves with their betters by talking about 'we,' the better for all parties." I said this in a scathing manner, and

feeling painfully warm in the forehead.

"You're talking about what you don't understand, sir," said the exciseman or the tide-waiter, or whatever he was. We're all in the same boat. Pray do you never say 'we' when talking of your master's shop?"

"Master's shop, sir?"

"Oh, I beg your pardon," said he, mockingly. "aren't you a cashier in a fur-shop?"

Shop! Fur-shop! I could have seen him—seen him—moth eaten.

"I'll tell you what I'm not, sir," I burst out, losing self-control, "I am not the man to put up with the con—foun—ded impudence of an obscure tide-waiter."

"Tide-waiter!" repeated the Beast, starting to his feet.

"Tide-waiter," I calmly reiterated.

At this, the whole family of the Nuttleburys, who had hitherto appeared to be paralysed, interposed, one screeching out one thing, another yelling another. But they were all—Mary and all—against me, and affirmed that I had purposely picked a quarrel with their relation—which, by-the-by, I rather think I had. The unpleasantness ended in Mr. Nuttleburry's requesting me, in so many words, to withdraw.

"After what has occurred there is nothing left for me, but to do so," I remarked, making towards the door with much majesty; but if Mr. Huffell thinks that he has heard the last of this, he is a good deal mistaken. As for you, Mary," I continued; but before I could complete my sentence I experienced a sensation of an elderly hand in my coat-collar, and found myself in the passage, with the room door closed against me. I lost no time in vacating this ignominous position, and seeking the open air. Presently I found myself at my desk writing to Dewsnap.

Dewsnap was then my greatest friend. He was, like me, in the fur business, and was a fine honourable upright noble fellow, as bold as brass, and always especially sensitive about the point of honour. To this friend I wrote a long account of all that had happened; asking his advice. I mentioned at the end of my letter that I was only restrained by the want of a pair of pistols, from inviting this wretched being to a hostile meeting.

The next day I passed in retirement, speculating much on what Dewsnap's answer would be. It was a day of heavy rain, and I had plenty of time to mourn over my exclusion from the cheerful abode of the Nuttleburys, and to reflect how much better off my rival was (sunning himself in my adored one's smiles) than I, a lonely exile, flattening my nose against the window of a country inn, and watching the drippings of the roof-drain as they splashed into the fast-filling water-butt. It is needless to say that I retired to rest early, and that I was unable to sleep.

I could sleep next morning, however, and did so till a late hour. I was aroused from a heavy slumber, by a loud knocking at my door, and the sound of a voice which I seemed to recognize.

"Here, Shrubsole! Hi, Oliver! Let me in. Shrubsole, what a lazy fellow you are!"

Gracious Heaven, was it possible? Was it the voice of Dewsnap? I rose, unlocked the door, and jumped into bed again.

Yes, it was my friend. He entered erect, vigorous, energetic as usual, deposited a small carpet-bag near the door, and, retaining a curious-looking oblong mahogany box under his arm, advanced to greet me.

"What on earth do you do lying in bed at this time of the day?" said Dewsnap, grasping my hand.

"I couldn't sleep till morning came," I answered, passing my hand athwart my brow. "But how did you get away?"

"Oh, I've got a few days' holiday, and am come down to answer your letter in person. Well? How's this affair going on?"

"Do not ask me," I groaned. "It has made me wretched. I know no more. You don't know how fond I was of that girl."

"Well, and you shall have her yet I'm going to settle it all for you" said Dewsnap, confidently.

"What do you mean to do?" I asked with some hesitation.

"Do? Why, there's only one thing to do?" He rattled the queer-looking mahogany box as though it contained metallic pills.

"What have you got in that box!" I asked.

"There's a pair of pistols in this box," said Dewsnap, proudly, "with either one of which it would almost be a pleasure to find yourself winged."

"Sir?" I observed, sitting up in bed with marked displeasure.

"You mentioned your difficulty about weapons, so I borrowed them of a friend of mine—a gun-maker—and brought them down with me."

"Hang him!" I thought, "how very prompt he has been about it. Amazingly prompt, to be sure.—You think, then," I added, aloud, "that there's no—no other way out of the difficulty?"

"Apology," said Dewsnap, who had now opened the box, and was clicking away with the lock of one of the weapons, with the muzzle directed towards my head—"ample apology on the part of the other side—is the only alternative. Written apology, in fact."

"Ah," I replied. "I don't think the other side will agree to that."

"Then," said my friend, extending his pistol, and aiming at a portrait of the Marquis of Gran-

by hanging over the fire-place : "then we must put a bullet into the exciseman."

(And suppose the exciseman puts a bullet into me, I thought to myself. So erratic is thought !)

"Where does the exciseman live?" inquired my friend, putting on his hat. "There is not a moment to be lost in these cases."

"Wait till I'm dressed," I remonstrated, "and I'll show you. Or you can go after breakfast."

"Not a bit of it. The people down stairs will tell me where to find him. Nuttlebury's, I think you said? I'll be there and back by the time you're ready for breakfast."

He was out of the room almost before he had done speaking, and I was left to make my toilet and improve my appetite for breakfast with the reflection that the number of such meals in store for me was, perhaps, more limited than I could have wished. Perhaps I a little regretted having put the affair into the hands of my energetic friend. So erratic (I may again remark) is human thought!

I waited some time for my friend, but was obliged at last to begin breakfast without him. As the meal was approaching its termination, I saw him pass the window of the little parlour in which I took my meals, and immediately afterwards he entered the room.

"Well," he said, sitting down at the table and commencing a vigorous attack on the eatables, "it is as expected. We are driven to extremities."

"What do you mean?" I asked.

"I mean," remarked Dewsnap, chipping away at his egg, "that the other side declines to apologize, and that consequently the other side must be howled down ;—shot."

"Oh dear me." I said—relenting, Major, relenting—"I shouldn't like to do that."

"You wouldn't like to do that? May I ask Mr. Shrubsole, what you mean by that remark ?"

"I mean that, that—is there no other way out of it ?"

"Now look here, Shrubsole," said my companion, with a severe air, and suspending for a moment his attack on the breakfast ; "you have put this affair in my hands, and you must allow me to carry it through, according to the laws of honour. It is extremely painful to me to be engaged in such an affair" (I couldn't help thinking that he seemed rather to enjoy it). "but, being engaged in it, I shall go through with it to the end. Come ! We'll get these things cleared away, and then you shall sit down and write a formal challenge, which I will undertake to deliver in the proper quarter."

Dewsnap was too much for me. He seemed to have all the right phrases at his tongue's end ;

he was so tremendously well-informed as to what was the right thing to do, and the right thing to say when conducting an affair of this kind, that I could not help asking him whether he had ever been engaged in one before?"

"No," he said, "no: but I believe I have a sort of aptitude for the kind of thing. Indeed, I have always felt that I should be in my element in arranging the details of an' affair of honour."

"How you would enjoy being a principal instead of a second!" I said—rather maliciously; for Dewsnap's alacrity aggravated me.

"No, not a bit, my dear fellow. I take such an interest in this affair that I identify myself with you entirely, and quite feel as if I *was* a principal."

(Then you feel a very curious sensation about the pit of the stomach, my boy, I thought to myself. I did not however give the thought expression. I merely mention it as an instance of the erratic nature of thought)

"By-the-by," remarked Dewsnap, as he pocketed my challenge and prepared to depart, "I forgot to mention that one or two fellows of our acquaintance are coming down."

"One or two fellows?" I repeated, in a highly displeased, nay, crushing tone.

"Yes, Cripps is coming, and Fowler, and perhaps Kershaw, if he can get away. We were talking your affair over, the evening before I left, and they were all so much interested in it—for I predicted from the first that there must be a meeting—that they're all coming down to see you through it."

How I cursed my own folly in having entrusted the keeping of my honour to this dreadfully zealous friend of mine! I thought, as he marched off erect and fussy with that wretched challenge in his pocket, that there was something positively bloodthirsty about the man. And then those other fellows coming down for the express purpose of seeing somebody shot! For that *was* their purpose, I felt. I fully believed that, if by any fortunate chance there should be no blood shed, those so-called friends of mine would go away disgusted.

The train of reflection into which I had fallen was interrupted at this juncture, by the appearance outside the window, of three human figures. These turned out, on inspection, to be no other than the individuals whose taste for excitement I had been condemning so strongly in my own mind. There they were, Messrs. Cripps, Fowler, and Kershaw, grinning and gesticulating at me through the window, like vulgar unfeeling idiots as they were. And one of them (I think it was Cripps) had the brutality to put himself into the attitude supposed to be the correct one for a duellist, with his left hand behind his back,

and his right raised as if to discharge an imaginary pistol

They were in the room with me directly, large noisy, and vulgar, laughing and guffawing—making comments on my appearance, asking me if I had made my will, what I had left to each of them, and otherwise conducting themselves in a manner calculated to turn one's milk of human kindness to bitterest gall. How they enjoyed it! When they learned that Dewsnap was actually at that time away on a war mission, and that he might return at any moment with the fatal answer—I say when they heard that, they positively gloated over me. They sat down and stared at me, and every now and then one of them would say, with a low, chuckling giggle, "I say, old fellow! How do you feel about it now?" It was a hideous relief to me when Dewsnap returned with the baleful news that the challenge was accepted, and that the meeting was appointed for the next morning at eight o'clock.

Those ruffians enjoyed themselves that afternoon to the utmost. They had such a pleasure in store for next day, that it gave an added zest to everything they did. It sharpened their appetites, it stimulated their thirst, it imparted to the skittles, with which they amused themselves during the afternoon, an additional charm. The evening was devoted to conviviality. Dewsnap, after spending some time in oiling the triggers of the pistols, remarked that now they were in such prime condition, that they would "snap a fellow's head off, almost without his knowing it." This inhuman remark was made at the moment when we were separating for the night.

I past the greater part of the dark hours in writing letters of farewell to my relations and in composing a stinger for Miss Mary Nuttlebury, which I trusted would embitter the whole of her future life. Then I threw myself on my bed—which was not wholly devoid of knobs—and found for a few hours the oblivion I desired.

We were first on the ground. Indeed, it was necessary that we should be, as those three ferocious Anabaptists, Cripps, Fowler, and Kershaw, had to be stowed away in places of concealment whence they could see without being seen; but even when this stowage had been accomplished and the fatal hour had arrived, we were still kept waiting so long that a faint hope—misgiving, I meant to say—began to dawn in my heart that my adversary had been seized with a sudden panic, and had fled at the last moment, leaving me master of the situation, with a bloodless victory.

The sound of voices, and of laughter—laughter—reached me while I was musing on the prospect of an honourable escape from my perilous position. In another moment my antagonist, still talking and laughing with some one who closely followed him, jumped over a stile at the side of the field in which we awaited him. Grinning in the most impudent manner, my antagonist inquired of his second, who was the village apothecary's assistant, whether he was a good hand at patching up bullet wounds?

It was at this moment that an accident occurred which caused a small delay in our proceedings. One of the Anabaptists—Cripps—had, with a view to concealment, and also perhaps with a view to keeping out of harm's way, perched himself in a tree which commanded a good view of the field of action ; but not having used sufficient caution in the choice of his position, he had trusted his weight to a bough which proved unequal to the task of sustaining it. Consequently it happened that just as the seconds were beginning their preliminary arrangements, and during an awful pause, the unlucky Cripps came plunging and crashing to the ground, where he remained seated at the foot of the tree in a state of undignified ruin and prostration.

After this there was a prodigious row and confusion. My opponent having thus discovered that there was one person observing our proceedings from a place of concealment, concluded naturally enough that there might be others. Accordingly a search was promptly instituted, which ended in the unearthing of my two other friends, who were obliged to emerge from their hiding places in a very humiliated and crestfallen condition. My adversary would not hear of fighting a duel in the presence of so large an audience, and so it ended in the three brutal Anabaptists being—very much to my satisfaction—expelled from the field. The appearance they presented as they retired along the pathway in Indian file, was the most abject thing I have ever beheld.

This little business disposed of, there remained the great affair of the day to settle, and it took a great deal of settlement. There were diversities of opinions about every detail connected with the murderous operations. There were disputes about the number of paces which should separate the combatants, about the length of those paces, about the proper method of loading pistols, about the best way of giving the signal to fire—about everything. But what disgusted me most, was the levity displayed by my opponent, who seemed to think the whole thing a capital joke, sneering and sniggering at every thing that was done or said. Does the man bear a charmed life, I asked myself, that he behaves with such sickening flippancy when about to risk it ?

At last all these endless preliminaries were settled, and Mr. Huffell and I remained staring

defiance at each other with a distance of only twelve paces between us. The beast was grinning even now, and when he was asked for the last time whether he was prepared to make an apology, he absolutely laughed.

It had been arranged that one of the seconds, Huffell's as it happened, should count one, two, three, and that at the word "three" we should both fire (if we could) at the same moment. My heart felt so tight at about this period, that I fancied it must have contracted to half its usual size, and I had a sensation of being light on my legs, and inordinately tall, such as one has after having had a fever.

"One!" said the apothecary, and the monosyllable was followed by quite a long pause.

"Two !"

"Stop !" cried a voice, which I recognized as the voice of adversary, "I have something to say."

I whisked myself round in a moment, and saw that Mr. Huffell had thrown his weapon down on the ground, and had left the position which had been assigned him.

"What have you to say, sir ?" asked the inexorable Dewsnap, in a severe tone ; "whatever it is, you have chosen a most extraordinary moment to say it in."

"I have changed my mind," said Mr. Huffell, in a lachrymose tone ; "I think that duelling is sinful, and I consent to apologize."

Astounded as I was at this announcement, I had yet leisure to observe that the apothecary did not look in the least surprised at what had happened.

"You consent to apologize ?" asked Dewsnap, "to resign all claim to the lady, to express your deep contrition for the insolent expressions you have made use of towards my friend ?"

"I consent," was the reply.

"We must have it all down in writing, mind !" stipulated my uncomprising friend.

"You shall have it all down in writing," said the contrite one.

"Well, this is a most extraordinary and unsatisfactory sort of thing," said Dewsnap, turning to me. "What are we to do ?"

"It is unsatisfactory, but I suppose we must accept his apology," I answered, in a leisurely and nonchalant manner. My heart expanded at about this period.

"Has anybody got writing materials about him by chance ?" asked my second, in a not very conciliatory tone.

Yes, the apothecary had, and he whipped them out in a moment—a note-book of unusual size, and an indelible-ink pencil.

An apology of the most humble and abject kind was now dictated by my friend Dewsnap, and written down by the crushed and conquered Huffell. When he had affixed his signature to the document, it exactly filled one leaf of the apothecary's memorandum-book. The leaf was torn out and handed to my representative. At that moment the sound of the village-clock striking nine reached us from the distant church.

Mr. Huffell started as if the day were more advanced than he anticipated.

"I believe that the document is regular?" he asked. "If so, there is nothing to detain us in a spot henceforth replete with painful associations. Gentlemen both, good morning."

"Good morning, sir," said Dewsnap, sharply; "and allow me to add, that you have reason to consider yourself an uncommonly lucky young man."

"I do so consider myself, I assure you," retorted the servile wretch.

With that, he took his leave and disappeared over the stile, closely followed by his companion. Again I thought I heard this precious pair explode into fits of laughter as soon as they were on the other side of the hedge.

Dewsnap looked at me, and I looked at Dewsnap, but we could make nothing of it. It was the most inexplicable thing that the man should have gone so far, should have had his finger on the trigger of his pistol, should have waited till the very signal to fire was on the lips of his second, and should then have broken down in that lamentable manner. It really was, as my friend and I agreed, the most disgraceful piece of cowardice of which we had ever had experience. Another point on which we were agreed, was that our side had come out of this affair with an amount of honour and glory, such as is rarely achieved by the sons of men in this practical and un-romantic age.

And now behold the victor and his friends, assembled round the small dining-table at the George and Dragon, and celebrating their triumph by a breakfast! in preparing which all the resources of the establishment were brought into play.

It was a solemn occasion. The moment, I acknowledge, was to me a glorious one. My friends, naturally proud of their associate, and anxious to commemorate in some fitting manner the event of the morning, had invited me to this meal to be provided at their own expense. These dear fellows were no longer my guests. I was theirs. Dewsnap was in the chair—it was of the Windsor pattern—I was placed on his right: while at the other end of the table, which was not very far off, another Windsor chair supported the person of Mr. Cripps, the vice. The viands set before us were of the most recherché

description, and when these had been done full justice to, and the chair had called for a bottle of champagne, our hilarity began almost to verge on the boisterous. My own mirth, indeed, was chastened by one pervading thought, of which I never for a moment lost sight. Had I not a secret joy which champagne could neither increase nor diminish? Had not my rival formally abdicated, and was I not that very day to appear in the presence of Mary Nuttlebury as one who had risked his life for her sake? Yes. I waited impatiently for the hour when these good fellows should take their departure, determining that, the moment they were gone, I would take possession of the field ingloriously vacated by my rival, and would enjoy the fruits of my victory. I was aroused from these reflections by the voice of my friend Dewsnap. It was, however, no longer the familiar acquaintance who spoke, but the official chairman.

Mr. Dewsnap began by remarking that we were met together on an occasion and under circumstances, of a very peculiar—he might almost say of an anomalous—nature. To begin with, here was a social meeting—nay, a convivial meeting, taking place at ten o'clock in the forenoon. That was the first anomaly. And for what was that meeting convened? To commemorate an act belonging to a class of achievement, usually associated with a bygone age, rather than with that in which an inexorable Destiny had cast the lots of the present generation. Here was the second anomaly. Yes, there were anomalies, but anomalies of what a delightful kind! Would there were more such! It was—Mr. Dewsnap went on to say—the fashion of the day to decry the practice of duelling, but he, for his part, had always felt that circumstances might occur in the course of any man's career which would render an appeal to arms desirable—nay, to one who was sensitive on the point of honour, inevitable—and he therefore thought it highly important that the practice of duelling should not wholly fall into desuetude, but should be occasionally revived, as it had been on—on—in short, the present occasion.

At this moment, curiously enough, a faint cheer was heard in the distance. It came, doubtless, from the throats of some of the village-boys, and presently subsided. It was enough, however, to deprive our worthy chair of the thread of his eloquence, so that he was compelled to start again on a new tack.

"Gentlemen," said Mr. Dewsnap, "I must throw myself on your indulgence if my words fail to flow as freely as I could wish. I am, to begin with, gentlemen, powerfully moved, and that alone is enough to deprive me of any small amount of eloquence of which I may at other times be possessed. Likewise, I must frankly own that I am unaccustomed to public speaking at ten o'clock in the morning, and that the daylight puts me out. And yet," continued the chair, " I do not know why this should be so. Do not wedding-breakfasts take place by daylight ? And are not speeches made on those occasions ? And, after all, why should we not look upon this very meal as, to a certain extent, a wedding-breakfast ? You seem surprised, gentlemen, at this inquiry, but I will ask you whether the event we are met together to celebrate—the event of this morning—has not been the first act of a drama which we all hope will terminate in a wedding—the wedding of our noble and courageous friend !"

It was a curious thing that, just when our chairman had got as far as this in his speech, the cheering we had heard before was repeated; though now much more loudly. It was also a curious thing that the bells of the village church, which was not very far off, began to ring a merry peal. There might not be much to concern us, in this, but still it was curious. The attention of Mr. Dewsnap's audience began to wander, and their glances were, from time to time, directed towards the window. Mr. Dewsnap's own attention began also to wander, and the thread of his discourse seemed once more to elude his grasp.

" Gentlemen," he began again, resolved, like a true orator as he was, to avail himself of accident, " I was remarking that this festive meal was, in some sort and by a figure of speech, a kind of wedding-breakfast, and while the words were yet upon my lips, behold the bells of the village church break out into a joyous peal! Gentlemen, there is something almost supernatural about this. It is a happy augury, and as such I accept it."

The bells were becoming quite frantic now, and the cheering was louder.

" And as such I accept it !" repeated Mr. Dewsnap. " Gentlemen, I should not be surprised if this were an ovation offered to our noble and courageous friend. The villagers have heard of his noble and courageous conduct, and are approaching the inn to offer their humble congratulations."

It was quite certain that the villagers were approaching the inn, for the sound of their voices became every moment louder and louder. We all began to be restless under our chairman's eloquence, and when at length the sound of wheels rapidly approaching was added to the cheering and the bell-ringing, I could bear it no longer, and rushed hastily to the window, followed by everybody else in the room, the chair himself included.

A carriage and pair drove swiftly past the

window. Major, I sicken while I speak. There was a postilion on the near horse, and on that postilion's jacket was a—Oho!—Excuse me, I beg—a wedding favour. It was an open carriage, and in it were seated two persons; one, was the gentleman, who had made me that humble apology not much more than an hour ago; the other, was Mary Nuttlebery, now, if I were to believe the evidence of my senses, Mary Huffel. They both laughed when they saw me at the window, and kissed their hands to me as they whirled away.

I became as one frantic. I pushed my friends, who in vain sought to restrain me, on one side. I rushed out into the village street. I yelled after the carriage. I gesticulated at the carriage. I ran after the carriage. But to what purpose ? It was over. The thing was done. I had to return to the inn, the laughing-stock of the rude and ignorant populace.

I know no more. I don't know what became of me, how my bill at the inn was defrayed, how I got away. I only know that I am finally, hopelessly, and irretrievably under a cloud; that all my old companions, and my old habits have become, odious to me; and that even the very lodgings in which I formerly resided are so unbearable, owing to the furniture being impregnated with painful associations, that I was obliged to remove and take up my quarters elsewhere. This, sir, is how I came to occupy these rooms, and I may here mention—if indeed the testimonial of a blighted wretch is of any value—that I have no cause to regret my change of abode, and that I regard Mrs. Lirriper as a most unexceptionable person, laboring indeed, as far as I can see, under only one defect. She is A WOMAN.

VII.

HOW THE PARLOURS ADDED A FEW WORDS.

I HAVE the honour of presenting myself by the name of Jackman. I esteem it a proud privilege to go down to posterity through the instrumentality of the most remarkable boy that ever lived—by the name of JEMMY JACKMAN LIRRIPER—and of my most worthy and most highly respected friend, Mrs. Emma Lirriper, of Eighty-one, Norfolk-street, Strand, in the County of Middlesex, in the United Kingdom of Great Britain and Ireland.

It is not for me to express the rapture with which we received that dear and remarkably remarkable boy, on the occurrence of his first Christmas holiday. Sufficient it to observe that when he came flying into the house with two splendid prizes (Arithmetic, and Exemplary Conduct), Mrs. Lirriper and myself embraced

with emotion, and instantly took him to the
Play, where we were all three admirably entertained.

Nor, is to render homage to the virtues of
the best of her good and honored s x — whom,
in deference to her unassuming worth, I will
only here designate by the initials E. L.—that
I add this record to the bundle of papers with
which our, in a most distinguished degree, remarkable boy has expressed himself delighted
before re-consigning the same to the 1 fichus-
glass closet of Mrs. Lirriper's little bookcase.

Neither, is it to obtrude the name of the old
original superannuated obscure Jemmy Jackman, once (to his degradation) of Wozenham's,
long (to his elevation) of Lirriper's. If I could
be consciously guilty of that piece of bad taste,
it would indeed be a work of supererogation,
now that the name is borne by Jemmy Jackman
Lirriper.

No. I take up my humble pen to register a
little record of our strikingly-remarkable boy,
which my poor capacity regards as presenting a
pleasant little picture of the dear boy's mind.
The picture may be interesting to himself when
he is a man.

Our first re-united Christmas-day was the
most delightful one we have ever passed together. Jemmy was never silent for five minutes, except in church-time. He talked as we
sat by the fire, he talked when we were out
walking, he talked as we sat by the fire again,
he talked incessantly at dinner, though he made
a dinner almost as remarkable as himself. It
was the spring of happiness in his fresh young
heart flowing and flowing, and it fertilised (if I
may be allowed so bold a figure) my much-es-
teemed friend, and J— J— the present writer.

There were only we three. We dined in my
esteemed friend's little room, and our entertain-
ment was perfect. But everything in the establishment is, in neatness, order, and comfort,
always perfect. After dinner, our boy slipt away
to his old stool at my esteemed friend's knee,
and there, with his hot chesnuts and his glass of
brown sherry (really, a most excellent wine!)
on a chair for a table, his face outshone the ap-
ples in the dish.

We talked of these jottings of mine, which
Jemmy had read through and through by that
time; and so it came about that my esteemed
friend remarked, as she sat smoothing Jemmy's
curls:

"And as you belong to the house too, Jemmy,
—and so much more than the Lodgers, having
been born in it—why, your story ought to be
added to the rest, I think, one of these days."

Jemmy's eyes sparkled at this, and he said,
"So I think, Gran."

Then, he sat looking at the fire, and then he
began to laugh, in a sort of confidence with the
fire, and then he said, folding his arms across
my esteemed friend's lap and raising his bright
face to hers:

"Would you like to hear a boy's story, Gran?"

"Of all things," replied my esteemed friend.

"Would you, godfather?"

"Of all things," I too replied.

"Well then," said Jemmy, "I'll tell you one."

Here, our indisputably remarkable boy gave
himself a hug, and laughed again, musically, at
the idea of his coming out in that new line.—
Then, he once more took the fire into the same
sort of confidence as before, and began:

"Once upon a time, When pigs drank wine,
And monkeys chewed tobaccer, 'Twas neither
in your time nor mine, But that's no mack-
er—"

"Bless the child!" cried my esteemed friend,
"what's amiss with his brain!"

"It's poetry, Gran," returned Jemmy, shout-
ing with laughter. "We always begin stories
that way, at school."

"Gave me quite a turn, Major," said my esteemed friend, fanning herself with a plate.
"Thought he was light-headed!"

"In those remarkable times, Gran and Godfather, there was once a boy;—not me, you
know."

"No, no," says my respected friend, "not
you. Not him, Major, you understand?"

"No, no," says I.

"And he went to school in Rutlandshire——"

"Why not Lincolnshire?" says my respected
friend.

"Why not, you dear old Gran? Because I
go to school in Lincolnshire, don't I?"

"Ah! to be sure!" says my respected friend.
"And it's not Jemmy, you understand, Major?"

"No, no," says I.

"Well," our boy proceeded, hugging himself
comfortably, and laughing merrily (again in confidence with the fire), before he again looked up
in Mrs. Lirriper's face, "and so he was tremendously in love with his schoolmaster's daughter,
and she was the most beautiful creature that
ever was seen, and she had brown eyes, and she
had brown hair all curling beautifully, and she
had a delicious voice, and she was delicious altogether, and her name was Seraphina."

"What's the name of your schoolmaster's
daughter, Jemmy?" asks my respected friend.

"Polly!" replied Jemmy, pointing his forefinger at her. "There now! Caught you!
Ha! ha! ha!"

When he and my respected friend had had a

laugh and a hug together, our admittedly remarkably boy resumed with a great relish:

"Well! And so he loved her. And so he thought about her, and dreamed about her, and made her presents of oranges and nuts, and would have made her presents of pearls and diamonds if he could have afforded it out of his pocket-money, but he couldn't. And so her father—O, he WAS a Tartar! Keeping the boys up to the mark, holding examinations once a month, lecturing upon all sorts of subjects at all sorts of times, and knowing everything in the world out of book. And so this boy——"

"Had he any name?" asked my respected friend.

"No he hadn't, Gran. Ha! ha! There now! Caught you again!"

After this, they had another laugh and another hug, and then our boy went on.

"Well! And so this boy he had a friend about as old as himself, at the same school, and his name (for He _had_ a name, as it happened) was—let me remember—was Bobbo."

"Not Bob," says my respected friend.

"Of course not," says Jemmy. "What made you think it was, then? Well! And so this friend was the cleverest and bravest and best looking and most generous of all the friends that ever were, and so he was in love with Seraphina's sister, and so Seraphina's sister was in love with him, and so they all grew up."

"Bless us!" says my respected friend. "They were very sudden about it."

"So they all grew up," our boy repeated, laughing heartily, "and Bobbo and this boy went away together on horseback to seek their fortune, and they partly got their horses by favour, and partly in a bargain; that is to say, they had saved up between them seven-and-fourpence, and the two horses, being Arabs, were worth more, only the man said he would take that, to favour them. Well! And so they made their fortune, and came prancing back to the school, with all in pockets full of gold enough to last for ever. And so they rang at the parents' and visitors' bell (not the back gate), and when they tell was answered they proclaimed, 'The same as if it was scarlet fever!' Every boy goes home for an indefinite period. And then there was great holiday, and then they kissed Seraphina and her sister—each his own love and not the other's on any account—and then they ordered the letter ...

"Poor man!" said ...

"Into insert correct, Gran," ... Jemmy, trying to ... d resisting ... laughter, "and he was to ... mothers ... but the boys' dinner, and ... to ..."

cask of their beer, everyday. And so then the preparations were made for the two weddings, and there were hampers, and potted things, and sweet things, and nuts, and postage-stamps, and all manner of things. And so they were so jolly, that they let the Tartar out, and he was jolly too."

"I am glad they let him out," says my respected friend, "because he had only done his duty."

"Oh but hadn't he overdone it though!" cried Jemmy, "Well! And so then this boy mounted his horse, with his bride in his arms, and cantered away, and cantered on and on till he came to a certain place where he had a certain Gran and a certain godfather—not you two, you know."

"No, no," we both said.

"And there he was received with great rejoicings, and he filled the cupboard and the bookcase with gold, and he showered it out on his Gran and his godfather because they were the two kindest and dearest people that ever lived in this world. And so while they were sitting up to their knees in gold, a knocking was heard at the street door, and who should it be but Bobbo, also on horseback with his bride in his arms, and when had he come to say but that he would take (at double rent) all the Lendings for ever, that were not wanted by this boy and this Gran and this godfather, and that they would all live together, and all be happy! And so they were, and so it never ended!"

"And was there no quarrelling?" asked my respected friend, as Jemmy sat upon her lap, and hugged her.

"No! Nobody ever quarrelled."

"And did the money never melt away?"

"No! Nobody could ever spend it all."

"And did none of them ever grow older?"

"No! Nobody ever grew older after that."

"And did none of them ever die?"

"O no, no, no, Gran!" ...
boy, ...
...
"A ..."
...
...